Praise for Allie Boniface's
Summer's Song

"Assumptions, misconceptions, misguided actions on the part of main and secondary characters alike, ensure the reader will stay glued to the page to the end to unravel all the intertwining threads of mystery...Ms. Boniface's fluid writing and vivid imagery work as strongly on the scene setting as they do on her characters, and make for a clever and intriguing read. For me this book is a keeper."

~ *The Long and the Short of It*

"Allie Boniface's Summer's Song is an engrossing story about hidden pasts, lost memories, and finding love despite everything else...I thoroughly enjoyed this book, a wonderful read when you want to curl up on the couch and relax."

~ *Ecataromance*

Look for these titles by
Allie Boniface

Now Available:

One Night Series
One Night in Boston
One Night in Memphis
One Night in Napa

Summer's Song

Allie Boniface

A Samhain Publishing, Ltd. publication.

Samhain Publishing, Ltd.
577 Mulberry Street, Suite 1520
Macon, GA 31201
www.samhainpublishing.com

Summer's Song
Copyright © 2010 by Allie Boniface
Print ISBN: 978-1-60504-819-2
Digital ISBN: 978-1-60504-693-8

Editing by Deborah Nemeth
Cover by Amanda Kelsey

First Samhain Publishing, Ltd. electronic publication: November 2009
First Samhain Publishing, Ltd. print publication: November 2010

Dedication

For Damon H. and Rachel V., two of the real-life inspirations for this story. Thanks for friendship that lasts over the years and beyond the miles...

Chapter One

Summer stared at the solid silver container holding her father's remains. Funny. She'd always pictured someone's ashes preserved in some kind of fancy urn. Something sculpted or carved. Something meaningful. Dignified. Instead, Hope Memorial Services, following Ronald Thompson's wishes, had sealed his remains in a six-by-eight-inch metal box, which now sat in the center of Joe Bernstein's desk.

She pushed the rest of her father's life into a large manila envelope and slid back her chair. "I'm finished."

"You're sure you don't—"

"Joe." She held up one hand, fingers ringless and well manicured. "No. I don't need anything else." *Except to get out of Pine Point as soon as possible.* She smoothed her suit jacket and brushed the ridge of the engraved business card holder deep in her pocket.

Summer Thompson, Chief Curator, Bay City Museum of History. Knowing the words were there, close to her skin, brought relief. She could do this. After a brief look at the house and a meeting or two with a local realtor, she could hop a plane back home to San Francisco. Within the museum walls, her world made sense. She could catalog the lives of other people and draw conclusions about long-gone civilizations. She could organize press conferences, plan exhibit openings, and design educational seminars for the local schoolchildren.

Outside those walls? She lost her voice. She lost her grip. She couldn't puzzle together the last decade or fit together the fragments of her own life. And she damn well couldn't say the word *father* or utter the word *dad*. Ronald Thompson hadn't been one to her in over ten years. She pulled out her cell phone to check her messages.

"Actually, there's something else we have to talk about before you go."

"Sorry?" She pulled her attention back to Joseph Bernstein, the elderly, craggy-faced lawyer she'd known since childhood.

"I know you're planning on selling the place—"

"Of course I am. I don't know why he left it to me in the first place." *My father did what? Willed me the McCready estate?* She'd grown dizzy with the news, now almost a week old. Kids in town called the three-story mansion haunted and avoided it on their way to school. Teenagers broke into it, leaving empty beer cans and used condoms on its dusty floors. Adults ignored it, driving by its thick hedgerow without so much as a glance at the craggy black rooftop that speared the sky. Now it belonged to her in a nightmare she had yet to awaken from.

"...but that isn't going to be as easy as you might think."

"Selling it? Why not?" She glanced through the paperwork on the desk between them. "Is there some kind of lien? A problem with the property?" *Please, God, no.*

"Not really." He waited a moment before continuing. "But there's an old farmhouse on the back acre that your father rented out. Family's been living there for a couple of years now."

She put her phone away again. "You're kidding me. So if I sell, I'm a schmuck who's throwing someone out of their home."

"Just wanted you to know."

"Well, can I sell it with some kind of contingency? Let the renters stay on?"

"Sure, you could talk to the realtor about that. Might make it harder to find a buyer, though."

Great. Summer shifted in her chair.

"Mac Herbert's doing the repairs on the place," Joe said after a pause. "You remember him? Went to school around the same time as you."

She nodded.

"He's got a young guy, new in town, helping him out. Damian Knight. He and his family are the ones renting the farmhouse."

"Wait—they're still working on the house? Who's paying them?" She hadn't expected the place to be in the throes of renovation.

"Your father made arrangements. Left a checking account with enough money to cover materials and labor."

"Really?" Every day revealed a new surprise, another piece of information she didn't know about her father. One week and she was already exhausted with the effort of trying to make sense of them.

The white-haired man leaned forward on his elbows. "You want 'em to stop? We can list the place as is."

She shook her head. "I don't—I guess I'll have to go out and see before I say one way or the other." She knew nothing about selling houses or about renovations that might or might not make a difference to potential buyers. *One more thing to think about. Terrific.*

"And you're sure you don't want to do a memorial service, or..."

"No." What on earth would she say to people? Who would

11

come to such a thing? She hadn't spoken to her father in ten years, since the accident. Everyone in town knew that. If they came, they'd only stare. "He's the one who chose cremation," she added. No headstone in the local cemetery, even though—

She stopped the thought before it could turn into something ugly. *Don't come back here,* Ronald Thompson had grunted into the phone years ago. *No reason. Don't want to see ya.* So she hadn't. "No service," she repeated.

Joe reached over and squeezed her hand. He still wore the thick gold ring she remembered, encrusted with his initials and those of Yale Law School. "Sweetheart, don't rush. Take some time to think things through." He paused. "I'm worried about you."

Summer lifted her purse onto her shoulder. "Don't be." The manila envelope went into her briefcase. She adjusted the clip holding her midnight-black hair away from her face, then tucked the box of ashes under one arm.

He tented his fingers together. "How long're you staying?"

"I'm not sure. A few days, I guess. I'll go look at the house now, do what I need to tomorrow. Can't stay any longer than a week." She had museum exhibits coming in. A fundraising meeting the following Tuesday and an interview with the local paper the Thursday after that.

She couldn't put the rest of her life on hold just because her father had chosen June fifteenth to die.

June fifteenth. Tears rose in her eyes before she could stop them. God, the irony of it might have just about killed her if she'd let herself think about it for longer than a few seconds.

"You'll call me before you leave?"

Summer paused, one hand on the door. "You know I'm too old for you to worry about, right?"

The sixty-year-old rose, all knees and elbows inside a navy suit that hung the wrong way on his angular frame. "Never. Your father—"

Is dead, she wanted to say. She squared her shoulders. *And I don't feel any sadder today than I did all those years ago when he sent me away from Pine Point.* For a moment, an eighteen-year-old with flyaway hair, bright blue eyes and a stomach full of grief reared up in her memory.

"I'll call you later," she said instead, before Joe could say anything about finding serenity or forgiving or remembering the good times. She had gotten enough pity and prayers from the flower arrangements and sympathy cards that arrived in the mail. She thought she'd about drown in other people's tears. Death erased things, she wanted to tell all the well-wishers. It didn't preserve them, and it sure didn't peel back the edges of ten years of pain so you could examine it all over again. Death, expected or not, allowed people to move on. *In fact, it forces us to.* Why was she the only one who understood that?

She leaned on the heavy glass door of the Bernstein, Lowery and Samuels law office and gritted her teeth. She didn't want to walk down Pine Point's Main Street to the corner lot where she'd parked her rental car. She didn't want her designer heels to catch in the cracked sidewalk by Evie's Parlor, where the tree roots always came up, and she didn't want to get caught at the only red light in town while Ollie at the corner station pumped gas and whistled at her.

But neither could she stay in this office one more minute. Outside, at least, the sunlight might blind her enough to keep the ghosts from taking up residence inside her head again.

CSBO

Mac pulled his arm across his forehead, already damp with exertion. "She's coming to check out the house. I heard last night."

"Who is?"

"Summer Thompson. Ron's daughter."

Ah, the new owner. Damian leaned against the porch railing and scratched his head. "Guess you owe me twenty bucks, then."

Mac grinned. "Yeah. You called it right."

"I knew she would. No one'd be able to sell a place without even lookin' at it." He stuck his hammer into his tool belt, slung low across his waist. "What's she like?"

Mac took a long pull on his soda and thought for a minute. Lunch lay scattered on the steps around them, and he eyed a second sandwich before answering. "Christ, it's been a long time..."

"Not that long. And this town isn't that big. I'm betting you remember something."

"It's been ten years. Long enough. Lotta people have come and gone."

"You went to school with her, though, right?"

Mac nodded and reached for another can of soda. He cocked his head. "Actually, she was pretty cute back then."

"Yeah?"

"Kept to herself a lot, but yeah. Hot body, pretty face... Hey, quit hogging the chips." He grabbed the bag from beside Damian and dumped the crumbs into his mouth.

"Why'd she leave town?"

Mac busied himself with collecting cans and tossing them into a cardboard box. "Long story."

"C'mon. Fill me in."

The burly man shrugged. "Her little brother died in a car accident, week or so after she graduated from high school. Boyfriend was driving." He shook his head. "Damn awful thing. Her father sent her off to live with an aunt somewhere near Chicago. She never came back after that."

Damian whistled. "Guess I'm surprised she bothered now."

Mac stood with a grunt, one hand on his lower back. "Be too bad if she decides to sell the place, huh?"

"Why?"

He stared. "You know that house of yours is part of her property, right?"

Damian dug one heel into the ground. Shit. How had he forgotten? The farmhouse was a rental because they didn't have the money to buy a place outright. They never had. And his mother had just finished decorating it the way she liked. He slammed the porch step with a fist and swore aloud.

"Maybe she'll divide the property, sell the farmhouse to you."

"Yeah." And maybe pigs would get up on their hind legs and dance.

"Sorry, man." Mac clapped a hand onto Damian's shoulder. "Not a done deal, though. Talk to her when she gets here." He swiped a hand over his mouth. "If it doesn't work out, I got a cousin with a couple of rental places over in Silver Valley. You want her number, lemme know."

Damian nodded without answering. Despite the sun that scattered its rays over everything in sight, the afternoon had turned glum. He glanced over his shoulder at the mountains that rose just beyond the roofline of the McCready house.

About fifty miles west of the New York-Massachusetts

border, Pine Point hovered at the base of the Adirondack Mountains. To most people, it was only an exit off the interstate, a stop halfway between Albany and Syracuse where you could get some gas or a burger before continuing on to more interesting destinations. According to the locals, Pine Point got too much snow in the winter and not enough sun in the summer. Nine thousand people, give or take, made their blue-collar lives here, and about the only thing they seemed to like about the place were the ridges that surrounded it and caught the light at sundown.

Damian didn't care about any of that. He only knew that Pine Point had given his mother and sister a place to escape, a chance for a new life, and for that he'd been grateful. Now it looked as though the ground beneath them was about to be pulled away once more.

CB&O

Summer nosed her rental car, a white Mustang convertible, onto Main Street. Fifteen years ago Pine Point had installed its first and only traffic light. Now she could see that they'd added another, past the library. Slowing for the red, she braked and looked around. *A few changes, not many.* The town had some new stores, the roads were in better shape and the city limits reached out a little farther. In the distance she caught a glimpse of a new housing development dotting what she remembered as farmland with paved roads and sprawling homes.

The light changed and a pickup truck behind her tooted twice. Raising her hand in acknowledgement, Summer squinted into the rearview mirror. Sure enough, she recognized the face at the wheel of the blue Dodge Ram. Back in high school, Billy Watkins had been the leader of the Pits, a group of kids who skipped every class except gym and lunch and spent their days smoking out by the baseball fields. True to form, the Billy of today clenched a cigarette in his teeth and puffed with a vengeance as he turned the wheel and headed away from her.

She readjusted clammy hands on the steering wheel and wondered who else she'd see. She hadn't left any close friends behind except Rachael Hunter. Everything and everyone else had pretty much faded with the years. *Thank God.* A new café at the end of the block surprised her, and the sign above Alan Bros. Upholstery had a fresh coat of paint. She slowed for a gaggle of prepubescent girls who skipped across the street and disappeared into Doug's Dairy De-Lite. So far, so good. No bad memories. As long as she stayed on this side of town, it should stay that way.

But then her car slipped past the block of stores and neared Pine Point Central School, and against her will memories shimmered inside her head. A wide, white smile, broad shoulders that filled out a football jersey in all the right ways, a warm mouth that moved its way with painful, perfect slowness down her neck. She swallowed. Hard. With little effort, she could almost see Gabe Roberts again—eighteen, baby-faced and handsome enough to bring a lump to her throat. Bare skin against hers. Lips murmuring promises into the small of her back.

And then.

His voice, too high and panicked. His hand tugging at hers. Shrieking tires and metal thundering against metal. Moonlight and blood and then, finally, darkness. Gabe had been there the night everything changed.

Summer's jaw snapped shut and she bit the inside of her cheek. *Stop it. It happened forever ago. And it wasn't your fault, anyway.*

A car backfired as she reached the end of Main Street. Here

the houses spread farther apart and the sidewalks vanished. She took a deep breath and eased the Mustang to the side of the road. To her right, a hundred yards away, a wall of thick green shrubbery rose up, parted in the middle by a broken sidewalk. Spires shot into the air above the trees, and a lump grew in her throat. All thoughts of Gabe Roberts vanished in the shadow of the McCready house—monstrous, terrifying and all hers.

Chapter Two

"Oh my God." The words fell from Summer's mouth before she could stop them, and the steering wheel grew rubbery in her grip.

In front of her sat the McCready estate, larger and more imposing than she remembered. And more run-down, from the looks of it. Three stories skewered the sky, topped by cupolas and a widow's walk. The two upper floors boasted crumbling balconies, and ivy obscured many of the windows along the ground floor. A worn, chipped sidewalk led up to the porch, which extended the entire length of the house and wrapped around both sides. Beside it oaks and elms thrust their laden arms upward. According to the deed, the estate included five acres of property with the two-story farmhouse out back as well.

The rental house. Where that family lives. The pit in her stomach grew. Even after his death, Ronald Thompson hadn't managed to make things easy on her. "Couldn't just leave me a place I could put on the market right away, could you?" Summer closed her eyes for a moment and tried to summon strength. When she opened them again, she felt better. A little.

Through the hedges that separated the property from the street, she spied piles of lumber and building supplies strewn about the yard. Well, her lawyer had been right about that—the workers were definitely here and definitely in the middle of things. It looked as though a few trees had been trimmed and the roof replaced, but that only made the peeling paint and cracked windows look more pathetic. A lonely house, three times bigger than the one she'd grown up in, and it waited for her with empty, echoing rooms.

Oh, Dad. What the hell were you thinking?

She glanced at her watch and climbed from the car. Part of her—most of her—wanted to hop on a plane and fly straight back to the other side of the country. Out there, she knew who to trust and who to avoid. She had an apartment, a career, a routine to fill her days. And high school lay tucked away in a neat row of photo albums on the top shelf of her closet.

"Ow! Dammit, Damian, watch it—what the—"

"Sorry, Mac."

Well, the men were still here, anyway. Maybe she could talk to Mac and his assistant about what the place needed and how much she could expect to get if they stopped renovations right now.

Summer followed the sidewalk through the hedges and scraped both bare arms on her way through. A trickle of blood appeared on her elbow and she wiped it away. *Mental note: at least have them trim these suckers.* As she pushed her way into the front yard, the walk ended and she tripped over rough ground. *And fix the sidewalk too.* Wouldn't do to have potential buyers lining up at the emergency room after taking a tour of the place.

"Hello?" Despite the scaffolding propped against the front of the house and the tools scattered everywhere, the grounds seemed vacated. *I just heard them...* "Mac?"

"I thought I said—"

She looked up. There, along the roofline, stood two men.

The head on the right bobbed up and down. A thick arm jabbed skyward for emphasis. She smiled as she recognized the bushy-haired, no-necked running back from Pine Point High's football team. She shaded her eyes. Next to Mac, another head with lighter hair caught gold from the sun. She didn't recognize it.

"I'll take care of it."

"Well..." Mac's voice faded, and Summer couldn't hear the rest of his reprimand.

She cupped her hands around her mouth and sent up another greeting. For a moment no one responded. Then both men leaned over the edge of the roof and stared down at her.

"Summer?"

"Hi, Mac."

The man wiped his brow. "You're earlier than we—hang on. We'll be down in a minute."

Summer nodded, but they had vanished. As she waited, she took a few more steps toward the house. The double front doors hung loose on their hinges, the glass inside them scarred and cracked. Ancient graffiti scratched illegible names in the wood. The porch was scuffed and scarred, and dusty cobwebs decorated every corner. *What a mess.*

She ran one finger along the splintered banister. Even run-down and raggedy, though, the house stood with a sort of grandeur. If she closed her eyes, she could almost picture a woman in hoop skirts sweeping her way down the wide stairs while a man in a top hat and tails waited for her at the bottom. *Maybe I could do some research on the place, find out its history.* People liked buying a house with a story.

"Hey, you can't go up there." A strong hand grabbed her elbow.

"What?" Summer shook her arm free. *This is my house*

21

now, she wanted to say. *I can go wherever I want.* "Why not?"

"Not safe yet." He motioned to the steps, and when she looked closer, she saw the space left by a missing riser gaping like a placid crocodile and ready to snatch up her unsuspecting foot.

"Oh." She smiled an apology at Mac's helper.

He was tall with light brown hair and deep blue eyes, and his broad, shirtless chest shone with sweat. Muscular biceps, no doubt made strong from summer labor, twitched as he reached for an itch between his shoulder blades. Summer swallowed and tried to chase away a crazy urge to scratch the spot for him.

She cleared her throat and shook the hand he offered. "I'm Summer Thompson. The—ah—the owner of this place."

He studied her with a serious expression. "So I guessed. Damian Knight."

The one who's renting the farmhouse. "Listen, I—" She meant to talk to him about it, but a heavy hand landed on her shoulder, and she turned.

"Summer!" Mac Herbert stood beside her, half an inch shorter and a good deal wider than she. All muscle. "Can't believe you're here." He shook his head and grinned, and Summer glimpsed the chipped front teeth she remembered from high school.

"Well, I wanted to see the house. I just..." She faltered. "I just found out about it."

His expression sobered. "I know. Your father wanted it to be a surprise for you. Sorry about your loss, by the way." He looked over his shoulder. "He did a great thing, buying this place. Wish he could have seen it finished."

She didn't think it was a great thing at all but she kept her mouth shut. Maybe someone else would find beauty in it. Maybe someone else would want the story that came with owning such an estate.

Mac gestured around the yard. "We're finishing up the roof today. And the top floor needs reinforcing. Don't use the front steps, 'kay? Gotta replace a few."

"It looks..." *Like nothing I would ever want to live in? Like the biggest mistake my father could have made?* She wasn't sure what to say.

"It's a helluva lotta work," Mac interrupted her thoughts. "But your father paid us through Labor Day, and we'll probably finish most of the major work by then. I got a few guys who'll help out with the interior when we get there. Course, I don't know what your plans are. If you're gonna sell it, or..." He stopped and waited for her to finish the sentence. She didn't.

"Can I see the inside?" Summer asked instead. She wanted an idea of the mess she was dealing with. Her doubt grew as she looked around. Forget the plans her father had made for repairs. She couldn't see dumping a lot of money into the place.

Mac shrugged. "Sure. I can show you the main floor, anyway. Second and third floors too, though there's not much up there." He glanced at his watch and turned to Damian. "You're leaving early today, right?"

"Yeah." But Damian didn't move. Instead he ran one hand through his hair and sent a cloud of sawdust flying. A grin touched his eyes and, for a brief second, Summer saw her own reflection in his gaze. She looked small and dark, a little girl floating on the blue of his iris. He smiled, and in the sunlight, the blue deepened until she felt like she was falling inside it, floating, forgetting who and where she was. Something jumped in her stomach, and her palms tingled. Knights in Pine Point? There hadn't been any for as long as she could remember.

Don't fall for the guy whose heart you have to break tomorrow.

Mac cleared his throat. "Uh, there's a door around back we can use until these stairs are fixed."

"Okay." She negotiated the grass-stubbled walk, following Mac and ticking off her to-do list inside her head. Her heels sank into the soft grass in spots, and she almost lost her balance and tumbled over a pile of shingles.

Stupid, she thought for the tenth time that day. *Stupid idea to come back here at all.* With her eyes on the ground, she managed to reach the far corner of the house without losing her footing again. Then she made the mistake of turning and peeking over her shoulder. Damian had pulled on a faded red T-shirt, which promptly turned damp and stuck to him in all the right places. He bent and collected some tools, and his chiseled arms flexed as he deposited them into a box. He vanished through the shrubbery, and a few minutes later the roar of a throaty car engine signaled his departure.

She shook her head and reached for the wobbly banister of the back porch. *Stop it. He's a local guy working on the house, that's all. So he's got a great body. And an amazing smile. He's still nothing to get worked up over. You'll be gone in a matter of days.*

And he'll be packing up his things and moving, courtesy of your signature on a sheet of paper.

The thought kept her going even as it ached inside her chest and made her sorry for someone she'd just met.

CB&O

"...and that's it," Mac finished.

They stood on the landing between the first and second

floors. Little air moved inside the house, and the humidity seemed to have skyrocketed in the last half hour. Summer pulled her hair off the back of her neck. Begrudgingly, she admitted her father had been right to buy the property. Even in the places where the moldings, the doors, the stairs would have to be replaced, Mac promised he could do so and be true to the design of the house.

Dwarfed by impossibly tall walls and a ceiling rimmed with ornate, crumbling crown molding, she turned in a slow circle and took it all in with her curator's eye. Who had lived here a century ago? The lady of the house, preening before a gilt-edged mirror as she waited for guests to arrive? Her husband, who toiled over the books by candlelight? Had five or six children tumbled across the threshold? Had an army of servants kept it spotless? She made a mental note to visit the archives down at the Town Hall and see what she could unearth about the history of the house. It would definitely help the sales listing.

She glanced into a good-sized bathroom off the main hallway. A claw-foot tub stretched along one side, and built-in cabinets covered one whole wall. Maybe she should let them continue remodeling. It would increase the value of the place, that was for sure. She took in the cathedral ceiling, the grand foyer below her, the bedroom to the right and the great room to her left. *The second floor would make a nice master suite and a good place to...*

Summer stopped breathing.

From where they stood she could see straight through the great room's tall windows. Thickets of pines surrounded the house, with a cloudless sky above them. Beyond the trees, a mile or so away, rose a solid black fixture. For a moment, her eyes watered and she couldn't see anything at all. Then she took a deep breath and fastened her gaze on the main gate of All Saints' Cemetery, resting place for just about everyone who spent their lives in Pine Point.

Goose pimples rose on her arms as she understood exactly why her father had bought this house. Somewhere in that green expanse, a few hundred yards away, lay her brother's remains. Her hand lifted to her mouth before she realized it, as if to keep the thoughts in her head from leaping out.

This had nothing to do with me. He didn't want me to live here. He just wanted to bring me back to Pine Point so I could stand in this spot and remember what happened that night. Resentment drilled into her heart. She'd never stepped foot inside All Saints'. She had no idea where her brother was buried or what his headstone said. Her father had never bothered to tell her. Now he wanted her to live within shouting distance of it?

"Summer, listen carefully. Can you hear me? Do you understand what I'm telling you?"

She rolled her head against the pillow. Everything hurt, from the bandage around her forehead to the splint that held her broken ankle in place.

"Aunt Sue is coming tomorrow to take you to her place. You'll stay with her out in Chicago for a while."

"But—"

"No buts. I've already decided. It'll be better for everyone..."

In a flash, the walls closed in on her. Darkness spiraled inside her peripheral vision. Summer couldn't breathe. That conversation—she didn't remember having it. She didn't remember anything from the night of the crash or the three days following. She blinked and stared into the distance until the curlicues at the top of the cemetery gate blurred. *What was that? What's happening?* Wiping both hands against her skirt, she fought the anxiety. Perspiration covered her forehead. *Get me the hell out of here.* She turned to flee but the heel of one Manolo Blahnik caught on the top riser.

"Whoa!" Mac caught her elbow and hauled her upright. "Might want to wear some different shoes if you're going to be hanging around here."

"Don't worry," Summer said through clenched teeth. "I'm not." She counted to ten and drew a breath. Then another. With shaking fingers, she wiped her forehead.

"You okay?" He stared at her.

"Yeah. Just the heat, I guess. It got to me."

"Here." He handed her a clean rag from a pile on the stairs, and she pressed it to her face, closing her eyes so she wouldn't have to see the pity in his gaze.

"Thanks."

"So what do you think?" Mac asked as they descended the stairs.

What do I think? Summer shook her father's voice from her mind and dropped the rag into a box. "I'm putting it on the market. Today, I hope." *It was some kind of weird flashback, that's all.* A shrink had told her she might experience them once in a while. She just hadn't thought coming back to Pine Point would jog the past into her present quite so quickly.

"Let me know if I can—I don't know, help out or anything," Mac offered.

"Thanks." By the time they reached the first floor, the memory was gone. "Any chance you know Sadie Rogers' number?" She needed to get this house listed, get it out of her hands as quickly as possible. She'd figure out how to deal with the complication of Damian Knight and his rental property later.

"There's a phone book in the kitchen." Mac checked his watch. "Might be tough to catch her, though. It's already after four."

Of course. Sadie owned the only real estate agency in town. She was also a single mother of twins and, according to Rachael, headed up both the PTA and the local Girl Scout troop. Mac was right. By the time Summer made her way across town, the doors to Rogers' Real Estate would be locked up tight. She pulled out her cell phone. "Well, let me call her, at least." If she couldn't get the paperwork taken care of soon, she'd be stuck here for longer than a few days.

"Staying at the Point Place Inn?"

Summer nodded. It wasn't as though the town boasted a slew of choices. Though she would have been welcome at Rachael's, she wasn't sure she could deal with the memories that would greet her there. Better a neutral hotel room with no connection to her past. She flipped through the thin local phone book and dialed Sadie's number. The answering machine at Rogers' Real Estate picked up, and she rattled off a quick message. With any luck, the woman would call her back tonight or early tomorrow. The two of them had gone to school together, even shared some of the same classes their junior year. Maybe Sadie could rush things along, work out the details over the phone, arrange for Summer to fax her signature from the West Coast.

Mac pulled a rag from his pocket and wiped his hands. "Well, if you need anything else, ah, or have questions about the place, gimme a call. Or just stop by."

"Okay. Thanks." She checked her voicemail. Four messages, none crucial. Good thing. Her brain, already on overdrive, couldn't handle much more this afternoon.

"I've got to go into town for some supplies," Mac said as he headed for the front door. "You're welcome to stick around if you like. Just be careful. You have a key?"

"Joe gave me one." Mac left, and Summer turned in a slow circle and surveyed the kitchen. A bay window looked out onto the back lawn, a green expanse that stretched to a grove of pine trees about a hundred yards away. She could imagine a breakfast nook here, a small table with chairs pulled up close and a checkered cloth on top. In her imagination, chattering children tugged on their mother's legs while she laughed over their heads to her husband. *A family belongs here. A family with lots of kids and lots of hope and no heartache.*

Summer waited a beat to see if her father's voice would echo inside her head again. When it didn't, she smiled. *Ghosts, that's all. Just my mind making things up.*

She pushed open the torn screen door and wound through the boxes on the back porch. She made her way down the steps and had almost reached the ground when her foot hit another soft spot. *Damn designer heels.* She grabbed for something— found nothing—stumbled and fell. "Oof." Her knees met the ground and she wrenched her wrist trying to break her fall.

"Son of a bitch." She kicked off both shoes, disgusted with herself.

"Hey, are you okay?" The voice came out of nowhere.

Terrific, a witness for her humiliation. She didn't answer, hoping the voice—and the person it belonged to—would go away. It didn't. Instead, a hand touched her shoulder. She jumped.

"Summer?"

Damian. Something loosened in her stomach and she scrambled to her feet. "I thought you were gone." She dropped a quick glance at his left hand. No ring. But carpenters didn't

29

always wear rings on the job, did they?

"Forgot something."

His hand had moved from her shoulder but it left an imprint of heat, a sort of strange desire, from the five fingers trailing their way along her neckline. She shivered despite the eighty-degree temperature. Her wrist ached and she cradled it, more to keep her hands from reaching out and touching him in places they probably shouldn't.

"Sure you're not hurt?" He took a step closer and bent to inspect the wrist she was rolling back and forth.

Summer shook her head and tried to find words. Her skin burned at his touch.

He rubbed it lightly, feeling the bones and massaging the tendons. "Doesn't feel broken."

"I...I'm sure it's fine. Just having a clumsy moment."

Damian smiled. "You get a look at the place?"

She nodded. Her arm still tingled from where he'd touched it.

"It's beautiful." Squinting, he leaned back as if to take it all in. "You can almost picture how it'll look, done." He met her gaze. "Your dad had a lot of vision. I'm sorry I didn't get a chance to know him better."

Summer bent to brush dirt from her skirt and didn't answer. It would take a lifetime to explain her relationship with her father to someone who hadn't always lived in Pine Point, who hadn't known the way her father had protected her. Worried over her. Blamed her and sent her away after her brother died.

"Listen, about the rental house," she began.

He stuck his hands into his back pockets. "Yeah. About that."

"If I can, I'll try to sell the place to someone who'll leave it status quo."

"And if you can't?"

She didn't answer.

"I get it. If you're selling, you don't have a lot of choices."

"I'm trying to figure them out. Really."

He nodded. "Guess I'll see you around."

The grass didn't feel so bad between her bare toes, and she leaned into it for a moment. "Yeah, guess so." Reluctantly, she slipped her shoes back on. "Leaving early for a hot date?"

"You could say that."

She raised her brows and felt again his strong, gentle fingers on her skin. *Of course he is. Look at him. Probably every woman in town wants to go out with him.* "What's her name?" Maybe she'd graduated with the woman.

Mystery clouded Damian's eyes. "Dinah."

"Oh." She didn't recognize the name. "Well, have fun."

"I will." He backed around the corner of the house, holding her gaze longer than he needed to.

Summer watched until Damian disappeared into the shadows. A long breath escaped her. On the surface, Pine Point seemed the same sleepy hamlet she'd grown up in, but when she looked closer, certain details had shifted in the last decade. A house that towered to the sky. A handsome, complicated stranger who turned her thoughts inside out. Memories of her brother and father that sprang up when she least expected them.

Suddenly exhausted, she headed for her car. She couldn't wait to get out of here.

CঞৎO

Theo Braxton drew a sleeve across his mouth and wiped away lunch. "You got 'em?"

Randall Potts, dime-store private investigator, nodded. He slid an unmarked manila envelope across the scarred desk and smiled. "Eight pictures. Taken last week."

Theo stared at the envelope without reaching for it. His foot jounced on the stained linoleum, nerves getting the better of him. Six years. He'd lived without them for six long years. And now he couldn't get up the balls to look at what the PI had uncovered. He coughed. "Got any water?"

The man with the hair plugs and cheap blue suit pushed himself up and ambled down the hall. Alone, Theo inched closer to the desk. Closer to the envelope. His heart hammered. He'd wanted this, after all. He'd convinced himself it was the right thing—the only thing—to find his wife and daughter and bring them home again.

Randall Potts returned with a paper-cone cup of water. "Here you go." He cleared his throat and remained standing. "That'll be two hundred, like we agreed."

Theo barely heard him. He downed the water in a single gulp and then slid one finger under the flap of the envelope. Eight glossy photographs slid into his hands, and there she was, his beautiful Hannah, smiling down at their daughter as the two of them ate ice cream at some roadside stand. Faint lines had etched themselves around her mouth and eyes, but he'd smooth them away. He'd make her remember what it was like to be young and carefree. Just bring them home again, and he'd give her anything she wanted. The moon or more. His groin swelled with want, and sweat broke out on his brow.

"Here." He handed over four fifty-dollar bills, fresh and uncreased. "When can you get me her address?"

The investigator cleared his throat. "You want that, I'll need another two hundred."

"Are you fucking with me?"

"Said you wanted pictures. You want contact info, it's gonna cost more. She's got a prepaid cell number and an unlisted landline. Tougher to trace."

"So just tell me where the pictures were taken." He could make out pine trees behind them and a cloudless blue sky. No buildings.

"You got the cash?"

Theo fisted both hands in his lap so he wouldn't reach over and throttle the guy.

"Got a roofing job next week. I'll have it then."

"Call me in ten days. You have the cash, I'll have what you need."

Theo got to his feet and slammed the office door on the way out. He was sick of waiting. Sick of wondering where they'd gotten to and how long until he could see them both again. Outside, he lit a cigarette and stomped to his truck. Probably should find out if his boss had any work for him, but all he really wanted was to belly up to E&J's bar for a couple shots of Jack Daniels.

He pulled out of the parking lot and cut off a mom in a minivan. She honked and got the finger in return as the shingle with Randall Potts' name on it disappeared in his rearview mirror. His temper eased. *Yeah, all right.* He'd give this idiot ten days, and if the guy couldn't deliver, he'd go to someone who could. Or he'd hunt down his wife and daughter on his own.

Chapter Three

Damian coasted to a stop outside the soccer fields by the high school. A few hundred yards away, miniature figures in bright yellow and red jerseys darted across the grass. Behind them, the sun hung over the hills and cast sheets of light in every direction. His watch read four forty. Good, he wasn't late. He drummed his fingers in a restless pattern on the steering wheel, basked in the silence and let his aching back relax. Closing his eyes for a minute, he listened to the faint shouts from the field. The images of soccer players faded, replaced by luminous dark eyes and blue-black hair.

Summer Thompson. From Mac's accounts, he'd expected her to be attractive. What he hadn't expected was someone with such a steady gaze, such long legs and a mouth that seemed to carve the air into intricate patterns when she spoke. She wasn't beautiful in the traditional sense, not like his ex-girlfriend or even one of the Hadley sisters, but something about the curve of Summer's lips and the lift in her chin made you stop and look. And then look again.

Damian opened his eyes and rubbed his face. No use getting worked up over her. She might be a looker, but she wasn't staying in Pine Point longer than a few days. Besides, he didn't have time for a girlfriend or even a fling. He wasn't available, and bottom line, Summer was the reason he might be homeless in a month.

A whistle blew. The players had gathered into a knot at the edge of the parking lot. Damian pulled himself from the Camaro and headed for the group. From here, they all looked the same—nylon jerseys and shorts, tall white socks and black sneakers. Hair pulled into ponytails on top of heads. Sometimes he tried to test himself, to see if he could spot Dinah before she saw him. He always failed. Sure enough, in another minute, she came running over.

"Dame!" Eight years old and tall for her age, his half-sister wrapped her arms around his waist and grinned.

"Hey, ladybug." Damian bent down and hugged her, damp hair and gangly arms and all. He tickled her ribs and she giggled up at him. God, he loved her.

"How was practice?"

"Good. I scored two goals."

"Great job." Damian smiled and looked over her head. Station wagons and mini-vans idled at the curb, and one by one the players climbed into their cars and waved goodbye. Dinah leaned into Damian's legs and watched them go, and his heart ached the way it always did. His little sister deserved better than this. She deserved a father who'd pick her up from practice and take her for ice cream, a father who'd come to her games and cheer from the sidelines. Most of all, she deserved a sober father who'd carry her on his shoulders and protect her from the darkness that waited around corners. Damian felt like a poor substitute most of the time.

"Let's go." Dinah pulled at her brother's hand.

"Dinah! Damian!" Petite and blonde, with breasts that always seemed on the verge of escaping her tiny T-shirts, Joyce Hadley jogged across the field.

Damian ignored her and reached for the car door. *Just*

pretend you didn't hear her. But Dinah tugged at his shirt.

"Dame."

"Hmm?"

"Coach Joyce wants to talk to you."

Damian resisted the urge to close himself in the car, roll up all the windows and take off without looking back. Instead, he took a deep breath, inhaled perfume and gagged.

In her matching sky-blue shirt and shorts, Joyce looked like she belonged on the cover of a fashion magazine rather than at the helm of a soccer team. She blushed and tucked her hair behind one ear with a pinky finger.

"Hi, Joyce. How'd my sister do today?"

The blonde fixed her gaze on Damian, barely looking at Dinah. "Fine."

"Anything I need to know about the game this weekend?" Damian rubbed an invisible spot on his shirt and stared at the ground.

"Be at the field by nine, same as usual."

Joyce glanced at Dinah and took one step closer to him. A gold cross dangled in the low-cut vee of her shirt. "We'll be at Murphy's tonight. You and Cat should stop by." Smooth pink lips whispered the invitation, and at her words his heart and his groin struggled against each other. He nodded and turned away without answering.

As Damian turned the key and pulled away, Dinah leaned out the open car window and waved. Joyce stood in the driveway beside the school. One hand twisted her hair; the other fluttered in their direction. She didn't move, even as they turned the corner and headed for home. He reached over and tweaked Dinah's ponytail.

"Why don't you like Coach Joyce?" Dinah propped both feet

on the dashboard and turned to her brother. Damian slowed as the light turned red and tried to decide how to answer the question.

"Dame?"

"What, ladybug?"

"Why don't you like her? She's always saying hello to you, and you never want to talk to her."

"I like her fine. She seems like a good coach."

"Yeah, plus she's pretty," Dinah continued. "And she bakes really good chocolate chip cookies."

"So you told me." *If that were all it took, I'd date her in a second.* But baking skills and good looks only counted for so much. Once you started peeling the layers away, you found out the truth about a person. All the truth, ugly and whole and real. After the heartbreak of Angie, he had no interest in dating. He couldn't bear to fall again, only to have the world pulled out from under him. Besides, Dinah and his mom needed him at home. Even if he'd wanted one, a relationship with Joyce Hadley wouldn't fit into his life.

"I wish I had hair like that," Dinah said after a minute.

"Hair like what?"

"Like Coach Joyce's. Long and blonde. Don't you like it?"

Damian grinned and pinched his sister's nose. "I like your hair. I like brown hair, black hair, even." A vision of Summer with ebony strands blowing across her eyes undulated in his mind for a moment. Yeah, he liked black hair just fine.

He turned just before the McCready place—or rather, the Thompson place now—and wound down a long dirt driveway. A minute later their barn-red house appeared. As soon as the engine died, Dinah jumped out and ran inside.

"Mom!"

Damian took his time before he followed her. He straightened the flowerpots that vied for attention on the porch steps and picked up stray bits of paper. When they'd lived in Poisonwood, his mom had kept a perfect house with blooming vines tumbling over each other and a fountain in the front yard. Ever since the divorce, though, she hadn't been the same. Doctors called it depression, but Damian suspected that the beatings she'd endured for years at the hands of her ex-husband hadn't helped. Still, since the move to Pine Point almost three years ago, she seemed better. The dark circles under her eyes had faded, and she didn't worry so much about letting Dinah leave the house.

Damian climbed the stairs and opened the screen door. Silence greeted him. The door at the end of the hallway stood closed. He stopped outside it and listened carefully. Nothing. Continuing down the hall, he ducked into the kitchen to find Dinah elbow-deep in chocolate ice cream.

"Want some?" A spoon dripped brown spots onto the faded linoleum at her feet.

"Ice cream before dinner?" Damian winked. "Sure, ladybug. Give me the works." He stuck one finger into the open container of whipped cream and dotted her nose with it. Dinah squealed with pleasure. When she dug the spoon into the carton again, he backed away and knocked on his mother's door.

"Mom?"

Damian pressed his ear to the door. "Mom? You okay?" Worry slid cold fingers up his spine. *When did the son become the parent? After T.J. started hitting Mom, when I was thirteen years old and barely big enough to fight back for her? After the divorce, when she spent twenty hours a day locked in her room sleeping? Or after we moved to Pine Point and she couldn't walk down the street without looking over her shoulder?*

He knocked again, and when he still heard nothing, he gripped the knob and wiggled it. This time a soft shuffling moved across the room. A moment later the door opened slowly, and Hannah Knight peeked out at him. Relief melted the tension at his temples.

"You're okay."

She smiled. "What's all the hammering about? Of course I'm okay. Can't a woman have a moment to herself?"

Without answering, Damian leaned in the doorway and studied her. Dark hair untouched by gray swung against her shoulders; faint pink circles touched her cheeks. Even the pain and loneliness that sometimes creased her countenance could never hide the huge eyes, the high cheekbones, the translucent skin. If only he could erase the emptiness that sometimes shadowed her expression and replace it with the easy, dimpled smile he remembered from years ago.

Hannah raised one hand to his face. "You've turned into such a handsome man," she said softly. "What happened to my little boy? Sometimes I don't even recognize you." She smiled. "I catch myself thinking, what is that good-looking guy doing in my house? You must drive the women in town wild."

He shuffled his feet. "No women for me, Mom. You and Dinah are the only ones I need."

She sat on the edge of the bed. "Oh, no. Don't be silly. You need someone besides us, besides this house. What about Dinah's soccer coach?"

Joyce? God, no. She can't take a hint. Won't leave me alone. He shrugged. "I don't know."

"It's been a long time since you and Angie broke up."

Damian winced. He knew.

"I want you to be happy."

"I am happy."

She rose and walked across the room. At the far window, she looked back at him. "You know what I mean."

He shrugged again. Angie was gone, Joyce didn't interest him and he didn't have the strength to bare his soul to anyone new. Suddenly Summer Thompson's face flashed into his imagination, and again he felt her wrist under his fingertips. He rubbed the back of his neck. *Where the hell did that come from?* His cheeks warmed.

"Listen, the new owner of the property stopped by today."

"And?"

"And she's talking about selling everything, this place too."

His mother's face lost its radiance. "There's no way we can stay?"

"I don't know. I'm gonna talk to her about it."

Hannah nodded and Damian vowed to find a way to keep them in this house. They'd gone through so much in the last few years. He couldn't bear for her and Dinah to move again. He pressed a kiss to his mother's cheek and backed out of the room.

Dinah stood in the doorway of the kitchen. She held a spoon in one hand and wiped her mouth with the other, leaving a streak of brown down the length of her arm.

He laughed. "You're gonna need a bath."

"Uh huh." She beamed up at him. "Hey, you wanna go for a hike before dinner? Mom said I could pick some of those flowers down by the creek, but she won't let me go alone."

Of course she won't. She's still too afraid T.J. might show up. Though the divorce had been final for years, with sole custody of Dinah granted to Hannah Knight, their mother still lived in fear that her ex-husband would steal the girl away. He hadn't shown up. He hadn't called. But neither did they believe that the guy was gone for good. Damian's fists tightened. With a love of liquor and a smile that could sweet-talk the devil when he wanted it to, T.J. was a rattlesnake with a deadly bite. Since the move, Damian had made it his personal responsibility to make sure he never got close enough to his girls to hurt the air they breathed or the ground they walked upon.

ᘓᘉᘒ

Theo slouched in the chair and pulled a baseball cap over his eyes. He didn't need the damn librarian or the old guy next to him giving him an eyeful while he was pecking away at the keyboard.

His first Internet search turned up nothing. "Shit."

A young mother nearby frowned and covered her toddler's ears. "Excuse me," she hissed. "This is the *library*."

Didn't think it was the fuckin' circus, he wanted to say. He bit his lip instead and tried another search. This time he typed in Hannah's son's name. He scowled. Damian Knight had never been anything but trouble in the years Theo had put a roof over their heads. Wouldn't be surprised if he was the one who had told Hannah to leave in the first place. He scowled at the screen. No matter where the three of them had ended up, Theo was one-hundred-percent certain Damian still lived with his mother and sister, if not in the house with them, then somewhere close by.

This search turned up something. He glanced around and hunched as close to the computer screen as he could get. Damian's name appeared halfway down a list of graduates from a two-year college somewhere in upstate New York. Theo pursed his lips and jotted the name of the school on a scrap of paper.

The date was almost three years old, but he would guess Hannah hadn't taken the family too far from there. He hadn't tried to contact her in ages. She would have grown comfortable by now. Safe.

Theo shoved the piece of paper into his pocket and closed the web browser. He thought a minute and then shut down the computer completely. Next step: finding a map of New York. After that, he'd drive straight from center-city Baltimore to whatever podunk town Hannah and Dinah now called home.

Damian he'd worry about when he got there.

Chapter Four

Summer studied the papers strewn across the blue polyester motel quilt. After only twenty-four hours away from the museum, she felt dissociated and out of the loop. Later in the summer, their museum would have the rare opportunity to borrow a collection of artifacts recovered from the 1607 Jamestown colony. She ran a finger down the list of broken wine cups and cooking pots. She loved reading background material, reliving archeological digs that brought such finds to light. And yet all the documents in the world could never explain the most important things.

They couldn't explain why a young girl, on a particular day, might have chosen to mix corn and venison stew in her cooking pot. Or whether she'd learned the technique from a Potomac Indian woman or raised a callus on her finger as she stirred. Had she watched her mother nurse a newborn? Had she blushed and dropped her chin when a certain boy walked by?

Summer pushed the papers together in a heap. She reached for the glass of water on her nightstand and wished it held something much stronger. *I only like putting other people's pasts in order because I can't remember my own.* That's what an ex-boyfriend had told her once. She downed the water and wondered if it were true.

She'd been back in Pine Point for over a day and, aside

from the one dizzying moment in the house that afternoon, she hadn't experienced a single memory of that night. Not that she wanted to. Her eyes filled as she tried to remember her brother's face, his laugh, the way he teased her about being in love with Gabe. She couldn't. It had all become a fog, which was just as well. More than one therapist had told her she was better off not remembering anything about the accident. Selective amnesia they called it, the brain sorting out and banishing any traumas too painful to recall.

Summer pulled off her T-shirt and pink panties and flung both over a chair. The sheets, pilled but soft, she drew up to her chin. *Sleep,* she ordered. *A good eight hours of it, please.* The day, too long and too full of memories, had worn her out. Tomorrow morning she'd find Sadie Rogers and get the house on the market. A couple of days later she'd fly out. And the whole thing would be over.

⋘⋙

Damian settled himself into one of the faded lawn chairs on the front porch and stretched out his legs. Folding one hand behind his head, he stifled a yawn and studied the mountains that wrapped their arms around the town. At night, especially in the absence of a moon, they became shadowy giants that towered over the residents. After almost three years of living in Pine Point, he still couldn't decide whether they soothed him or scared him. Sometimes he suspected it was a little bit of both.

The phone rang. Two minutes later Dinah appeared, framed in the doorway. "For you." She held out the receiver. "It's Catfish."

"Hey, Cat. What's up?"

Damian's best friend belched loudly into the phone. "We

going out tonight?"

"I don't care. Sure. Where?"

"Murphy's?"

Joyce Hadley flashed into Damian's mind, pink and sky-blue and smiling with eyes that wanted much more than to coach his kid sister. *We'll be at Murphy's tonight...*

"No. No way."

Cat belched again. "Well, where else?"

"How 'bout Jimmy's? I'll meet you there around nine."

"Sounds good."

"I'm going out with Cat for a little while," Damian told his mother a few minutes later.

"Good." Hannah smiled over the dishes she washed, though her expression seemed weary. "There's no reason for you to sit home with us every night."

But I would. He didn't need to say the words; they hung in the kitchen above them all, understood.

"We'll be fine," Hannah said, and the set of her mouth confirmed her words. "Go."

Out of habit, Damian checked the deadbolts on the front and back doors before he left and made his mother promise not to open the door for anyone except the police. She nodded, slipping into her quiet nighttime mood, and Dinah waved goodbye from her beanbag chair by the television.

With the day behind him and food in his stomach, Damian felt rested and more relaxed than usual. He tapped the steering wheel as the music poured from his speakers. He headed down Main Street toward the highway until he reached a side street just beyond the overpass. Cat stood outside Jimmy's Watering Hole, waiting. A corner bar away from the center of town, the place attracted the local thirty-somethings more than the drunken college kids home on summer break. *Much better than Murphy's.*

Damian had never really been into the bar scene, though he'd done it enough when he first started college. But one too many nights of wandering home near dawn and puking into a cracked dormitory toilet bowl had turned his stomach. Now he only went out occasionally, usually to quieter bars or the ones with a good band playing. Tonight the place was more crowded than usual, though, and he wondered if even Jimmy's had been a mistake.

"Thanks." He took the beer Cat bought him and shoved his way through the narrow room until he reached the back wall. Before him, a sea of faces blended together. He finished his beer in a few long swallows and propped the empty bottle on the table beside him. A collection of other bottles sat there next to a wrinkled cocktail napkin with a smeared phone number scrawled across it.

Damian worked his hands into his pockets. He was getting too old for this sort of thing.

The door to Jimmy's flung open and three—no, four—women pushed their way inside. Clad in too-tight T-shirts and miniskirts, they strutted across the room and winked at the bartender. Damian's chest tightened. The Hadley sisters—Tara, Joyce, Eva and Marie. All blonde, all beautiful. According to Cat, they'd grown up in Pine Point, two years apart in age, and never left. Damian wondered if they ever would. What the hell were they doing here?

He glanced over his shoulder and wondered if Jimmy's had a back exit. Nothing but bodies stuck too close together. Damn. He shrank into the wall and looked at his feet.

"Damian!" She'd spotted him.

His stomach did a slow flop, over and back, and he raised

his chin. No use avoiding her. "Hi, Joyce."

The tallest and blondest of the four wound her way through the crowd, and heads turned as she passed. When she reached him, Joyce looked up through mascara-drenched lashes and shook her head with a teasing smile.

Damian cleared his throat. "Thought you were going to Murphy's."

Joyce moved closer and bumped him with one hip. "Changed our minds. Besides, I thought you might show up here." She tucked a strand of hair behind one pierced ear. "You're with Cat?"

Damian nodded.

"Why don't you both come back to the house?" She curled an arm through his and pressed her breast against him. Warmth from her skin seeped through his shirtsleeve and into the crook of his elbow. It felt good, and for an instant he considered her offer. Maybe his mother was right. Joyce was easy on the eyes, and she sure wasn't making things tough for him.

Then he took a deep breath and shook his head. "Sorry. We're just on our way home, actually."

"Liar." Joyce pushed her lips out in a pout.

He shrugged. "I've got a lot of work to do tomorrow." That, at least, was true.

She released his arm and pouted a moment longer. "I'll be around if you change your mind. And you have my number." With a wiggle of her slim hips, she rejoined her sisters at the bar.

Damian watched her for a minute and then searched for his friend. In the dark ocean of faces and beer bottles, he couldn't see anything at first. Then he spied Cat at the other end of Jimmy's, leaning against the only window in the place. One of Joyce's sisters was giggling into his shoulder. Well, at least one of them would get lucky tonight. He threaded his way to Cat's other side and mumbled a goodbye.

"You're leaving already?" Cat pulled himself away. "We just got here."

"Long day."

"Call me tomorrow, then."

"Yeah, all right."

Eva Hadley started snaking her tongue along Cat's earlobe right about then, so Damian slid out the front door before Joyce could bury her fuchsia nails into his own skin and drag him home with her.

On his way back into town, he circled through Park Place Run, Pine Point's answer to Fifth Avenue. Cat told him there used to be cornfields here, as far as you could see in every direction. He had a hard time picturing it now. Seemed a shame to lose so much countryside, but he supposed everything changed in the name of progress. Now, instead of fields, sidewalks of red brick wound into darkness, and white lights dotted miniature trees in a crooked connect-the-dots pattern.

He slowed the car. One restaurant remained open and a few people sat at the bar. Suddenly Damian longed to be part of a couple just for one night, to sit at a bar and drown in a woman. To watch her cheeks darken and her skirt shift as she crossed her legs. To lose himself in her conversation as evening became midnight and then wound its way to dawn without taking a breath. He hadn't felt that way in years. Sometimes he thought he might not ever feel that way again.

CʒƏ

Summer sat up, no closer to sleep than she had been twelve hours earlier. Naked, she strode into the bathroom and rifled through her overnight bag. Nothing. She'd used up her last Ambien on the flight here. Not even a lousy Tylenol PM lay loose in the bottom of her bag.

She stared at her reflection. Dark hair, dark eyes, dark circles beneath them. A decent body, thanks to five days a week at the gym and curves that had emerged sometime around the tenth grade. She pulled her hair away from her neck. If she looked closely enough, though, she could see the scar along her collarbone. It mirrored the smaller ones on her left arm, the ones that crawled up the inside of her wrist, spider-web fashion.

Or broken-glass fashion.

She dropped her hand and let black locks cloak her face. She didn't need to look. She could trace the marks inside her mind.

Without warning, the dizziness started again. *Oh, God. No. I have to get out of here.* Sweat broke out on her forehead. She reached for her T-shirt, her jeans, a pair of flip-flops by the door. Car keys and purse. The walls wavered in her peripheral vision, and she had to brace herself with one hand. *Deep breaths,* she tried to tell herself but the oxygen seized up inside her chest and she started to wheeze.

"What's happening to me?" The words echoed inside the room and she stumbled against the wall.

"Summer? Where are you? I can't feel my legs. I can't—"

Summer yanked the door open and flung herself into the narrow motel corridor. The door swung shut behind her. A second too late, she patted her back pocket. No keycard for

49

Room 101.

"Crap."

It didn't matter now. His voice wouldn't disappear from inside her head. She began running down the hall. Her pulse jumped; she could feel it inside her wrists and at the base of her throat. Perspiration dotted her upper lip and the corners of her mouth, and she tasted salt. At the far end of the hall, just in time, she reached for the bar across the exit door and pushed. Hard.

"Summer? I'm scared. Where's Gabe?"

Sweet mountain air flooded her lungs, and the voice vanished.

Oh, God. She'd forgotten how good it tasted—or that air could even taste at all. A complex combination of pine trees and starlight and wet, steamy pavement fell onto her tongue. She skittered to a stop and looked up. There they were, the dark shadows that hugged Pine Point. They hadn't changed at all. They still stood, half-gorgeous, half-ominous, and looked down on her in silence. She remained there for long moment and just breathed.

Donnie. She laid one hand against her chest and willed her heart to slow. She hadn't dreamt of her little brother in years. She couldn't remember the last time she'd called up his voice inside her head. And yet just a moment ago, he'd sounded as though he sat right behind her, with anguish in his words. Tears filled her eyes and she pressed the heels of her palms to her face to stop them from coming.

"I have to get out of Pine Point." She'd been a fool to return in the first place.

I'll take a drive. Maybe that'll relax me.

Summer climbed into her rental and fumbled with the headlights. Ahead of her, at the end of Main Street, she saw the fading taillights of another car. Other than that, all of Pine Point looked deserted. She took the first left and followed Perkins Lane around the back side of town. Not much new here. She passed the same collection of low-slung homes and double-wide trailers set back from the road. Every other one had a basketball hoop hanging from its garage door and pots of impatiens on the front step. At the corner of Melody Lane she braked. Her mouth tasted chalky, and perspiration slid down her spine. *Of course.* She'd driven the familiar route without even realizing it. Her stomach turned over and she was glad she hadn't eaten much for dinner.

From here, she couldn't make out the one-story house with the sagging roof. She couldn't see the pine trees that grew together and closed in the windows. But she knew it waited, a short half-mile away. Her childhood home. The yard she'd spent so much time playing in, the stream she'd spent so much time digging around. She turned the steering wheel without pressing on the gas. She wanted to see. She didn't want to see. Daisy petals plucked themselves off the stem in her mind. Yes. No. Still she kept her foot on the brake. *Not tonight.*

"Wanna come over later?" Gabe's hand, warm on her bare thigh, moved upward. "Celebrate graduation?"

She cut him a glance. Not with my kid brother in the car.

"What?" Donnie's carrot-top head bobbed in the back seat. "What didja say, Gabe?"

"Shh." Summer turned up the radio. June-warm wind lifted the hair from her neck as the car darted along the empty roads outside Pine Point. She felt full, sated with the night and the

51

happiness of finally leaving high school and the thrill of the guy in the seat beside her. Yes, she wanted to spend all night with Gabe. All of tomorrow too, and every day of summer until they had to leave for college.

She hadn't known love could make her feel like this, like a helium balloon filled up to bursting. She adored him. And yes, she wanted to celebrate with him. God, more than anything. She wanted him to run his hands over her, to peel her clothes off the way he had last weekend when his parents were at the shore. But they had to take Donnie home first, or—

The other car came out of nowhere. Blinding lights. Grinding brakes. A snapping motion that engaged the airbag and bloodied her face. Tree limbs scratching at her arms and face. And the screaming, high-pitched and panicked in the dark.

"Summer? Summer?"

Something cold stiffened her spine. The voice came from somewhere over her shoulder, and she would have tried to see where, except she couldn't move her arms and she couldn't find her legs and all she could hear was her little brother looking for her—

Summer sucked in air and tried to stop her heart from leaping out of her chest.

"Why is this happening?" Her head dropped onto the steering wheel, and this time she gave in to the tears.

Stupid question. She knew the answer. Everyone in the town knew. Three miles from this spot, ten years ago, her world had shattered. Her brother—gone. The life she'd known— fractured. She'd spent a decade trying to piece herself together again, but being back in Pine Point was stirring her up in ways she'd never dreamed possible. Summer pressed her lips together to try to keep her weeping at bay. She tried to recall her brother, the other driver, what had happened when the cops arrived. She couldn't. She only remembered the blinding beam of a flashlight moving over the car. Sirens. Gabe's hand in hers.

And a lot of questions she couldn't answer.

Chapter Five

Summer eased her car into the last open space on the Hunter lawn, wondering again why she'd agreed to come to Rachael's lake party. She had no time for this. She had less than a week before she left Pine Point, and if she could work a small miracle, she'd be gone even earlier. No more dizzy spells or memories of the accident since the other night at the motel, thank goodness, and that one she was chalking up to fatigue. Still, fear laced the hours now.

"Summer!" Rachael Hunter waved from the front porch of the ivy-covered house.

Summer climbed from her car and looked toward the oak that hid the water. *I climbed that tree. I sat in the branches and spied on Cat and his friends until the sun went down.* How many days had she spent here, basking in the warmth of Rachael and her family? How many times had she fled the emptiness of her own home, left her father sitting alone while she tried to find a place to feel normal? And why hadn't she come back at least once in all the years since to visit her most loyal childhood friend? *Because I couldn't cope. Not even with seeing Rachael.* Suddenly she felt much older than twenty-eight. She palmed the car keys and locked the doors before she remembered she was in the middle of farmland, not downtown San Francisco.

"God, ten years, Summer. Look at you! I can't believe you're really here!" Rachael met her halfway and flung her arms around her best friend.

"Me either."

Rachael gave her a long look up and down. "You look good. Too thin, but good. How long are you staying?"

"Only a few more days."

"You're kidding."

"I have a ton of work at the museum."

"C'mon...you haven't been back here since high school. Can't you take some more time off? You're still running that museum, right? You're not dealing with anything that's going anywhere."

"Stop it." Summer bristled. She hated when people spoke about her job, about the way she'd chosen to spend her life, like that. As if centuries long gone were somehow less significant than what happened in the here and now. Without understanding the past, she always explained to the doubters, people had no business living in the present. Everything linked together in a beautiful, complicated chain.

"Sorry. I just mean that the exhibits aren't going to grow legs and walk away if you stay another week or two in Pine Point," Rachael added. "I've missed you."

"I've missed you too."

Rachael blew platinum blonde strands of hair from her eyes and handed over a plastic cup. "Well, I'm glad you're here now, anyway."

Summer sipped from the cup and gagged. "God, what is this?"

"Some punch Cat made. Why? Is it bad?"

She grimaced. "It's awful."

"Thanks a lot." A deep male voice spoke behind her.

She turned and stared. "Catfish?"

A tall twenty-five-year-old with white-blond hair identical to Rachael's grinned at her. "Hey, Summer. Welcome back." He paused and the playful light in his eyes dimmed. "I'm sorry about your dad."

She continued to gape at Rachael's little brother. "What happened to you?"

Cat's expression changed to puzzlement. "What do you mean?"

She waved a hand. "You're so...tall. When did you get all grown up?" When she left Pine Point, Catfish Hunter had been a cocky ninth-grader with acne and a bad haircut. Now he stood on the porch step below her, a man who'd grown about six inches and filled out.

He laughed. "Sprouted up in college."

"You look good." Summer shaded her eyes and remembered something else. "Do you go by Nathan now?"

Cat made a face. "Nah. I'll always be Cat. Nickname's too hard to break."

Rachael stole her brother's baseball cap and mashed it down on her head. "Besides, he still smells like a catfish. Don't you ever wear deodorant?"

Cat grabbed for the hat but his sister dashed inside the screen door and vanished. He shrugged. "Some things never change, huh?"

"I guess not."

He stood there a moment longer. "You're not staying long, are you? Here in Pine Point?"

Summer shook her head. "It's not my—I don't—" How did she answer? She wanted to ask how *he* could stay here after everything that had happened, but she supposed Donnie's classmates had survived better than his eighteen-year-old sister with a father who didn't want her around as a reminder.

Cat loped down the porch steps. "Coming to the lake?"

"Later." She waved and watched him disappear behind the oak trees, still amazed at the boy who had shed his awkward teenage skin for the shell of an adult. *He wears it well.* Still, he hadn't had much choice. When you lost your best friend at barely thirteen, the rough adolescent years that followed hardened you up a bit. Calloused you. Made you old before you really wanted to be.

Summer climbed the steps and let herself into the house. Inside the foyer sat the same smiling gnome doorstop. The same fruit-patterned wallpaper peeled in the corners of the kitchen. If she tried hard enough, she could almost smell the chicken casserole that Mrs. Hunter used to cook every Friday night. Summer leaned against the breakfast bar. Suddenly, she was twelve years old again, sleeping over at her best friend's house, playing hide-and-seek in the woods, sharing a tub of ice cream with Rachael and talking about boys in the dark, musty attic. "Where is everyone?"

Rachael sat at the dining room table munching on potato chips. "Mom dragged Dad to a quilt show over in Silver Valley. Everyone else is down at the lake."

"Oh." Summer exchanged Cat's punch for a diet soda.

"So what's it look like? From the inside, I mean." Rachael asked.

"What?"

"The McCready house. *Your* house."

"Oh, God. I don't know. It's a mess." She thought of the crumbling stairs, the broken windows, the cemetery gate visible from the second story.

Rachael straightened her brother's cap and propped her chin in one hand. "Remember when we used to go by there after school and dare each other to look in the windows?"

"Sure." Two skinny, knobby-kneed girls darted into Summer's memory.

"We never did, right?"

"Nope. We always chickened out."

"And now you own the place."

"So?"

Rachael shook her head. "You finally get to look in the windows. Get over your fears."

Anxiety dimmed the edges of her peripheral vision, and Summer's face flushed. She didn't answer.

"Summer Thompson?" The cop took her arm in his strong grasp. "Can you hear me? Can you tell me who else was in the car with you?"

She shuddered and drank the rest of her diet soda without stopping for a breath.

"Hey, you okay? You look weird."

"Yeah. Just tired." She didn't want to admit that the past was starting to pop into the present every time she turned another corner.

Rachael glanced out the window. "Oh, the guys are coming back in on the boat. Come on. I want to introduce you to someone." She pulled on Summer's wrist and dragged her outside.

"I don't really know if—"

"Don't say anything. Just let me introduce you. You'll like

him. He's cute."

"Rach, I'm only here for a few more days."

"And what?" Rachael parked both her hands on generous hips. "You can't have any fun in the meantime? Come on." She tugged on her arm again, and this time Summer didn't protest.

The roar of the boat engine grew as it coasted into the dock. In the boat, three bare-chested men held beers and laughed. A few hundred feet away, Cat reached an arm to help moor it.

Here at the edge of the lake, the lawn met the water's edge in a crooked dirt line. No beach, just some frizzled grass that merged with sandy pebbles and disappeared. From there Pine Point Lake took over, spreading one mile wide and three miles long, gorgeous and blue under the sun. The Hunters had their own dock, as did everyone who owned lakefront property. Two teams of laughing men and women played water volleyball nearby, and bikini-clad women sunned themselves on a raft moored a few feet away.

Summer shaded her eyes. How was it possible that this place still smelled exactly the same, like wind and water and suntan lotion? Put her anywhere in the world and pipe in this scent, and she'd be a teenager again, watching the sun beat down on Pine Point Lake. For a moment she froze, afraid that another memory would darken her mind. None did. She let out a breath of relief.

Rachael hopped from one foot to the other on the scalding wooden dock. "You guys ready to do some skiing?"

Two of the men in the boat glanced over. *Sure,* one mouthed over the engine's steady throb. He opened a fresh can of beer and lifted it in Summer's direction. *Hi there.*

Hi, she mouthed back. He was good-looking, a little portly but with muscular arms and a buzz cut that showed off his dimples. The second guy reached out a hand to help her in, and she took it. He looked familiar, and she guessed they'd probably gone to school together, maybe a few years apart. As he shoved some towels off a damp seat for her, she tried to recall the bright brown eyes and the laugh that started in his chest and moved down to his belly. *George Hoskin's little brother? Maybe—*

But then the third occupant of the boat turned around to say hello, and her thoughts scattered.

Damian Knight. The same wavy hair glinted in the sun. The same blue eyes lit up when he saw her. He raised one hand in greeting, and Summer waved hers in return. Her legs turned to Jell-O and she reached for the side of the motorboat to steady herself.

So Damian was one of Cat's friends. The one Rachael meant to introduce her to? A smile crept onto her face. She'd almost forgotten how people's lives wove themselves together in small towns, how everyone belonged to everyone else. Each person became a puzzle piece that locked together to make the town the living thing it was. No secrets here, and no strangers either.

"Hi again, Summer."

Rachael's eyes widened. "Again?"

"Damian's working on the house with Mac." *And lives on the property I'm about to sell.* Reality thudded against her heart.

"Oh, right. Forgot." Rachael took her place behind the wheel, revved the boat's engine and pulled the rope from the dock. The girls on the raft rolled over and waved as the boat passed. "So who's skiing?"

Summer stumbled as they accelerated across the lake. She sank into the seat directly across from Damian and tried to read his expression. Was he irritated she'd come? Resentful that she owned the place he rented? Or shaken just a bit by their legs so close together, the way she was? She slipped her sunglasses into place and stared across the lake. She'd talk to him later, make him see that she was looking out for both their best interests. She didn't think he'd mind moving. Renters knew houses might change hands over the years. Didn't they?

Rachael offered her the skis twice, but Summer shook her head. She was content to watch the others skim across the water's surface before they crashed into the waves and sucked in mouthfuls of Pine Point Lake. And she was more than content to watch the way Damian made them all look like amateurs as he cut in tight arcs across the boat's wake on a single ski.

Rachael laughed as she spun the boat in circles, trying to make him fall, and Summer relaxed in slow degrees. She'd been right to come. Some part of her had missed this tradition of early summer on the lake. She'd missed her best friend smiling, the laughter ringing on the wind, the houses rushing by. She'd missed the way an afternoon on the water turned to a night filled with bonfires and drinking until everyone's stomachs turned warm with alcohol and friendship and desire.

Summer ran her hands in the wake. After a while, Damian stretched out on the floor of the boat beside her, not speaking. Once he offered her a beer, and she took it. Their fingers brushed. Nothing touched but the space between them, yet the afternoon hummed with possibility.

CʒɃͻ

"Race you to the water!" Rachael shouted and pulled off her bikini top.

"Oh, God." Summer watched Rachael dart away and buried her face in her hands. Eight, eighteen, or twenty-eight, her best friend didn't seem to have a problem taking off her clothes.

Maybe that came from growing up on the water.

Dinner was over. Beer bottles lay scattered around the lawn. They'd barbequed over the open fire and toasted marshmallows as the sun and moon traded places in the sky. After dinner Summer had thought about driving back to the motel to work on some press releases, but two margaritas later she'd abandoned the notion.

A few others followed Rachael, and soon six or seven naked behinds bounced across the lawn and into the starlit lake. In another minute, the sounds of splashing and laughing echoed through the darkness. Summer smiled. True, some things never changed. There was something sensual about warm water splashing over bare skin. She'd tried skinny dipping a few times, but only on the cloudiest of nights, when Cat and his friends were far from the house. Tonight she had no intention of baring anything.

She sat on the bottom porch step and leaned back on her elbows. The bonfire smoldered close by and darkness wrapped her in comforting arms.

"Summer?"

She jumped.

"Sorry. Didn't mean to scare you." Damian materialized from the driveway and sat beside her.

"Oh." She let out a breath. "You didn't. Not really." She moved an inch or so away from him, distracted by the heat from his arm so close to hers.

"You're not swimming?"

"I do my swimming with a suit. And I forgot mine." Summer stuck her hands under her thighs. "What about you?"

He shrugged. "Not in the mood." He studied her. "Make any decisions about the house?"

"Ah, well, I'm trying, you know, to make sure..." She couldn't lie to him. Sadie had told her that selling the place with a rental contingency could take twice as long as without it. "I think you might end up having to move. I'm sorry."

He dug in the dirt with a stick. "We've been there for almost three years."

"Trying to make me feel guilty?"

His head snapped up. "No. Just saying."

"I'm sorry," she said again. "I know it's a lousy deal."

"Yeah." He paused. "You ever think about keeping it yourself?"

She kept her eyes on the grass. "Makes more sense to sell it. I mean, I guess my father bought it for me, but he made a mistake." *There's no way I could live in Pine Point again.*

She shifted on the step and wondered if the warmth on her cheeks bloomed from the fire or from something else.

"I'm sorry about your dad," Damian said after a minute.

"Don't be." She closed her eyes. "He wasn't...close to anyone. Didn't want to be. He had cancer for a while, a couple of years at least. But he didn't tell anyone until the end. He spent the last week in intensive care, over in Albany." She paused. "So I heard."

"You weren't in touch with him?"

"My mom died when I was really young, and Dad and I..." She took a deep breath. "We didn't talk after I left town."

"After your brother died?

Ah, so he'd heard the story. "Yeah."

Damian stretched out his legs. In the firelight, the blond hairs on his ankles glowed. "Can't imagine going through something like that."

"It was a long time ago."

"How old was your brother?"

"A week past thirteen."

He blew out a long breath. "Wow." He didn't ask anything else, and for that she was glad.

She reached down and picked up a twig, twisting it until it shredded. "That's another reason I have to leave. It's too hard to be here."

"I'll bet."

But Damian didn't know the worst of it, which was that now pieces of the night kept coming back when she least expected them to. She couldn't guess when the next anxious moment might strike, or the next corner of the past might peel away before her eyes. She was headed for a nervous breakdown unless she got out of Pine Point, and quickly.

She glanced over. "What about you? You didn't grow up around here."

"Nope. Try a place called Poisonwood, 'bout a hundred miles west of Philadelphia."

She wrinkled her nose. "There's nothing west of Philadelphia but farmland."

"Exactly. Which is why I think of Pine Point as a thriving metropolis."

Summer laughed.

"Oh, come on. It has a movie theater, two grocery stores, a separate elementary and high school...classy place, I'm telling you."

"Sure. Classy. So how'd you end up here?" It was a strange place to make a home if you hadn't been born in Pine Point. Single twenty-somethings—especially those who looked as good as this guy did—didn't exactly flock to its county seat.

His expression sobered. "Long story. Save it for another time, maybe?"

"Oh. Okay." Summer rose and inched her way toward the fire.

After a minute, Damian came to stand beside her. "What is it you do, anyway?" He held his hands above the flames.

She studied his fingers and the way they threw shadows in the dark. She thought of how he'd touched her with them, feeling her wrist after she fell, and a lump of desire rose in her throat. "I—um—I'm the director of the Bay City Museum in San Francisco."

"Mm...I don't think I've heard of it."

"Probably not. It's pretty small. But it has a lot of great artifacts from the nineteenth and early twentieth centuries—the Gold Rush, railroads, stuff like that. Plus we display traveling exhibits from all over the country."

Damian's eyebrows lifted. "Sounds like a cool job."

Her elbow brushed his, and electricity radiated up to her shoulder. "It is. I just love it. I could spend hours reading about the past—lost civilizations, cities and empires and the way one person, or one event, changed everything..."

"I know what you mean. Makes you wonder how different our lives would be if, say, just one thing had ended up different. If the South had won the Civil War. Or JFK had lived. Things like that."

Summer stared at him. "Exactly." The same crazy wonderings about the world kept her up many nights. She'd flip through the archives at work and think, *What would the world be like if we were still a colony of the British Empire?* Or she'd stare at a piece of needlework in its glass case and wonder about its creator. *Who were you, really? Did you love? Did your heart ache at a sunrise? What was the world like, then?*

65

A breeze lifted the hair at her neck, and she shivered. Faint shouts floated up from the lake. The flames burned lower.

"Course, present day has its moments too," Damian said. "Tomorrow, next week, next year, all this is history too. Keeps shaping itself while we're just passing through."

"I know. But somehow it's different when you're living in the middle of it."

He cocked his head, and Summer wondered if she'd said something wrong.

"You involved with someone back home?"

Her heart skipped inside her chest. "No. I mean, I was dating a guy a few months back, but—"

Damian caught her mouth with his before she could finish the sentence. She lost her breath as his hands wound themselves in her hair, and she staggered against him, tingles in her palms. He smelled like soap and sawdust and the faint spice of aftershave. She ran her hands along his biceps, iron beneath her fingertips. Something inside her wanted to peel away his T-shirt and feel skin against skin.

Their tongues met and one hand slipped from her hair to the small of her back. She could feel him against her, his want hard and making her own grow in waves the longer they stood there. After a long moment, he moved his lips to her cheek before resting his forehead against hers.

"I've wanted to do that since yesterday."

"Yeah?" She laughed, a ragged, breathless sound in the silence. "Trying to make me change my mind about the house?"

He pulled away from her and frowned. "No. Is that really what you think? "

"I was kidding."

He stuck his hands in his pockets and backed away. "Sure

about that?"

"Damian, please. I didn't mean—" Somehow she'd ruined things. Her mouth ached with the absence of his.

"Listen, I should probably go. Early day tomorrow."

"Wait. Let's talk about this. Please." But he was gone without even a glance over his shoulder.

Summer crossed her arms as disappointment flooded her. Sparks jumped in the dying fire, and a piece of wood toppled into ash. For a few minutes, she thought maybe he'd come back and let her explain. She'd been joking. She'd just made a stupid comment to fill up the nervousness inside her stomach. He'd see that. Wouldn't he?

But Damian didn't return. After a while, Summer laced her hands behind her head and stared at the stars. Maybe her father had been right. Maybe the farther away she went from Pine Point, the better for everyone.

Chapter Six

Sunlight poked its yellow fingers through the blinds and prodded her awake.

"Summer?" Rachael rapped on the door of the guest room.

"Mmph." She rolled over. "What time is it?"

"Little after ten." Her friend sat on the edge of the bed and began to bounce.

"You let me sleep that late?" She sat up, disoriented.

"Figured you needed it. I thought a party and conversation with a certain good-looking someone would be good for you." Rachael crossed her legs. "So? Tell me what happened last night."

Clad in a tank top, Summer tossed off the sheet, swung her feet to the floor and reached for her overnight bag. "What happened? I came to your party, had dinner, watched while you and some other fools ran around naked. Then I went to bed."

Rachael looked around the room. "So where is he?"

"What are you talking about?" Summer slipped off her shirt and pulled on a clean tank top and shorts. "Where's who?"

"Oh, please. Did you sleep with Damian?"

"Damian? What?" She shook her head, but the edges of a memory began to sharpen behind her eyes. Smiles over firelight. Damian's hand reaching across a step and touching hers. A heart-breaking kiss and a mistake on her part. Then nothing. "Of course not. I barely know him."

"Bummer." Rachael sighed. "That never stopped me, you know. Best way to get over sadness is a friendly little romp with someone who looks as good as Damian does."

"Well, I'm not you. And I'm not sad."

"Whatever. Did you at least kiss him?"

"God, do I have any privacy around you?"

"Not since I showed you how to use a tampon back in seventh grade, no."

Summer picked up her toiletry bag. She needed to fix her face, head back to the motel and meet with Sadie in less than an hour. She couldn't sit here with her best friend and debate the finer points of kissing Damian Knight. "I'm not telling you. Use your imagination."

"Geez, lighten up." Rachael vanished down the hall, and a moment later Summer smelled coffee brewing.

Summer ducked into the bathroom and splashed water on her face. *Take your own advice and stop thinking about him. So he kissed you. So what?* She pulled her hair back from her face and dabbed concealer on the circles beneath her eyes. She had more important things to worry about than the lips of the guy she was about to evict.

CRSO

Less than a half hour later, Summer rounded the curve in Sycamore Road. She adjusted the radio station and hummed along. "Ooh, don't you got what I need now baby..."

Damian's face popped into her brain. Again. *Makes you wonder how different our lives would be if, say, just one thing had changed...* Her cheeks grew hot and she had to tell herself to unclench her hands before she squeezed the steering wheel in two. Sometimes when she told people what she did, they looked at her as if she were crazy to dwell in the land of yesterdays and make her living among ghosts. But not this guy. He got it. The hairs on her forearms lifted at the memory, at his expression as he watched her in firelight.

She slowed at the stop sign where Sycamore met Main. A dangerous intersection shrouded by woods on both sides, this crossroads witnessed a few accidents every year as drivers blasted past the sign half-hidden by bushes. One winter when she was a child, a group of teenagers had collided with a snowplow. Four deaths, all under the age of eighteen. Pine Point had mourned for months.

"Summer? It's Donnie...I can't find him...I can't...Summer?"

Blackness. A sliver of moon. Stars that hung too low and burned her eyes when the blood ran into them.

"Summer?"

Can't find him? Summer blinked. That was Gabe's voice. She pressed one hand against her forehead and tried to catch her breath. *What does that mean? Were we looking for him?* That didn't make sense. They'd all stayed in the car until the cops came. Hadn't they?

Her hands shook. *Stop it. Stop thinking about it.* She pressed her lips together until she tasted blood. After a long moment, the thoughts and the voices receded again. But God, how long would it haunt her?

Today the sun blazed in the bluest sky and both roads stretched to the horizon without a car in sight. She forced herself to breathe. This was not the same intersection, and this was not ten years in the past. She was twenty-eight, stable and strong. She was not a girl lying in a hospital bed trying to understand why her brother wasn't standing beside her cracking jokes.

Summer turned right and headed for the motel. After her meeting with Sadie, maybe she'd try to find Damian at the house. She'd explain away her stupid comment of the night before. She could probably give him his last month rent-free to make up for the hassle of selling the property. Maybe that would calm him. Or convince him to kiss her. Or—

Out of nowhere, a red sedan careened into the lane in front of her. A horn blared. Summer choked on her breath, and adrenaline poured into her veins, triple-time. With her heart frozen, she stomped on the brake pedal and slammed it to the floor.

"What the—"

She didn't have time to honk her own horn or check her mirrors or wonder who the driver was or where he'd come from. With both hands clutching the wheel, she held her foot to the floor and prayed.

Time slowed. Every movement of her car seemed magnified a hundred times. The distance between them closed. She wasn't stopping fast enough. *Oh God.* She was going to hit the car square in its rear bumper. She glanced to her right. Could she pull off? Swerve around? Thick oaks lined the road, with almost no shoulder. The metallic tang of fear rose up on her tongue. The distance between her hood ornament and the red sedan narrowed to a few feet. Bracing herself for the impact, she bit her lip, and her back teeth ground together in panic.

Crashing glass and the blunt smack of metal against metal filled the air around her. Her car jolted to a stop. Then everything went silent.

Breath whooshed out of Summer's lungs. She'd smacked her funny bone against the armrest, and the tingling brought tears to her eyes. A sharp pain shot through her right ankle. The beginnings of a migraine began to pound behind her eyes. She tasted fresh blood and when she raised a hand to her mouth, she saw red.

For a minute, panic engulfed her. *I hit someone. Or maybe hurt someone.* She couldn't bear to look. She closed her eyes and counted to ten, then twenty. She heard nothing. After another moment, she forced her eyes open and ordered herself to breathe. *In. Out.* She wiggled her toes. All there, all accounted for. She touched her forehead, her chest, both arms. All okay. She eyed her car, assessing the damage. No cracks in the windshield. The hood seemed smooth, with no splintered metal.

Summer frowned. She *had* hit the other car, hadn't she?

Wait a minute...

As she looked around, she saw not the smashed bumper of her own convertible, but the dented bodies of two other cars, one the sedan, the other a large extended-cab pickup truck which had collided with it. Glass covered the road. Steam poured from the hood of the truck. Her own car had stopped after all, short of hitting either vehicle.

Relief made her hands shake all the same. When she was sure she could look without throwing up, she climbed from her car and stared at the mess in front of her. Silence. Skid marks. Horribly crunched metal. She closed her eyes for a brief moment. This stretch of road never saw much traffic, certainly not on a Sunday morning. She rubbed both temples and forced herself to squint at the sedan and truck. No one emerged from the car or truck. She took another look in both directions. No one was going to show up. She would have to deal with this on her own.

"Are you okay?" Rachael asked. Static on the phone buzzed her words into an echo.

Summer turned away from the accident scene and listened for the ambulance siren's wail. "I'm fine. Just a little shaken up."

"Do you want me to come down there? Wait with you?"

"No. Don't bother." She couldn't keep her eyes from returning to the two hunks of metal sitting in the middle of the road like injured monsters, unable to crawl away and hide themselves from the oppressive sun.

"Can you see anything? Do you know who it is?"

Summer shook her head before she realized she hadn't answered. "I don't...no." She couldn't bear to walk over there.

"Well, listen, call me later when you get back to the motel, okay?"

"I will."

As she hung up and tucked the phone back into her pocket, the first police car came screaming up the road from town. A rescue vehicle followed thirty seconds later. Behind them, a smaller pickup truck with a blue flashing light in the front windshield pulled to a stop. It parked perpendicular to the road, a few feet beyond the accident. Two men hopped from the truck and within a matter of minutes they had placed orange cones and lighted flares in a long, sweeping line.

Medics clambered over the scene like ants, attending to the sedan and pulling open the pickup's door. Summer leaned against the hood of her own car and licked her lips. *I should probably wait and give them some kind of statement.* After standing in the sun for nearly twenty minutes, though, her throat felt parched, and perspiration slid from her neck to the small of her back. One policeman took down plate numbers. The other walked over to her. She didn't recognize him.

"You the one that called this in?"

She nodded. "I was following the—" She pointed with a shaky finger. "The red car. Actually, it pulled out in front of me. I didn't see what happened. I didn't even see the truck coming from the other direction."

The officer flipped open a notepad and began to write. Her name? Address? Details of what she'd witnessed? Summer answered his questions as best she could and tried to avert her eyes as the medics pulled the unconscious driver from the truck's wreckage and loaded him into the waiting ambulance.

"Are they going to be okay?"

The officer glanced behind him. "Well, it's a nasty accident. Looks like the truck driver took the steering wheel and the windshield pretty good with his face. Couple broken ribs and a fractured nose, probably. Maybe a concussion too. Good thing you were following. They might have been out here for a while before anyone else came along."

Summer tried to nod. Right now she couldn't feel glad about that. All she wanted was to go back to the motel and get on with the rest of her day. She didn't have a strong stomach for blood. Or car accidents. "Do you need me for anything else?"

He shook his head. "Don't think so. I have your phone number, anyway, just in case." A yell from one of the other men interrupted him, and he turned away.

Summer wiped sweaty palms on her shorts and reached for her car door. Then she stopped. The man, the one who had yelled, jogged over to where the policeman stood. Dressed in his standard-issue blue shirt and pants, he looked like one of the many volunteer firefighters and medical technicians in town. Yet something about the way he crossed his arms and cocked his head made her squint. Hard. Then he opened his mouth and spoke.

"Dammit, it's Lonnie Perkins in the car. I went to school with him. He's banged up bad."

Lightning bolts jumped from the sky into Summer's skin. For an instant, the sunlight bouncing off the pavement distorted her view, but it didn't matter. The tugging in her heart knew, if her eyes weren't certain. Gabe Roberts—*her* Gabe Roberts, dark-haired and square-jawed, the boy she'd fallen in love with a lifetime ago—stood mere yards away. The pavement tilted beneath her feet. Her throat closed up. She stood there in the heat, frozen. *I don't—I can't—*

Gabe glanced past the policeman's shoulder and saw her. "Summer?"

She could only stand there and stare.

He ran the back of one hand across his brow. "Well, hi there." Three words rolled off his tongue, and a decade unfolded in a heartbeat.

"Hi."

He walked toward her with an uncertain smile, and for a minute she stood again in the sickly yellow light of Lou's Fifty Flavors ice cream stand as a brash teenage Gabe crossed the parking lot with his eyes on her. *Hi there.* He'd said the same two words back then, and she hadn't heard anything else the rest of the night.

"Welcome home." Something dark moved across his face, a shadow of something she imagined he saw on hers as well. "Sorry it's under such lousy circumstances."

Home. Is that where I am? Summer felt more like she'd tumbled down the rabbit hole, flown up to the moon, vanished into another dimension where everything upside down and backwards was now normal. She wondered if she were

75

hallucinating, or if the accident had thrown her into shock. After two or three years, she'd learned to put away the hurt of losing Gabe. And after two or three more, she'd forced herself to forget about him and move on. Only one scrapbook sat on a shelf back in her apartment, with pictures of their summer together and a few melancholy poems she'd scribbled when her father sent her away for good.

"Hey, you okay? You look a little—"

"I'm fine." Summer reached for the car to steady herself. "I just..."

Gabe nodded. "I know. Been working as an EMT for close to five years. Never gets any easier."

"You—you do this? All the time?" She stared at him. "How?" In God's name, after everything they'd been through, how?

He studied the man with the flares and didn't answer. "I heard you were coming back." He raised his gaze to meet hers. "Scared the shit out of me, you want to know the truth."

She could have asked why, but she already knew the answer. *Seeing you again makes it real. Reminds me of what happened. Makes my heart ache all over again.*

"You look good," he said after a minute. "Not so scary after all."

She laughed and lifted a hand to her hair. Strands had fallen and stuck to her cheeks. "So do you."

He shrugged.

"I sort of own a house here now," she went on.

"The McCready place."

"Heard that too?"

"You know how people talk." Kind eyes met hers and held them. "How long are you staying?"

"Only another few days. Long enough to list the place with Sadie Rogers. Then I'm heading back to San Francisco."

"Ah." The rescue truck roared to life. A lanky arm waved from the driver's side window, and the horn beeped. Gabe raised a hand in acknowledgement. "Guess I'd better go."

Summer nodded, not sure if relief or disappointment kept her from speaking.

"Do you..." His expression sobered. "Do you want to get together? Maybe have a drink or lunch or something?"

Her chest tightened. Peel back the layers of ten years? Make conversation about the present while the past sat on the table between them and waited for attention? The hazy flashbacks swarming her waking hours were one thing. Facing the one person who could bring them all to life was something else altogether.

Gabe spoke again before she could answer. "Never mind. Probably better we don't. I'm sure you've got a lot to do before you go back anyway."

Summer nodded as he walked away and thought that was the smartest thing anyone had said to her in a long time.

Chapter Seven

"Can I help?" Dinah perched on the curb as Damian unloaded bags of supplies from the trunk of the car. She jumped on first one foot and then the other, across the sidewalk and back.

"Not with this, ladybug." He juggled two bags of supplies and set them on the ground. Reaching inside the front door of the Camaro, he pulled out a smaller paper bag. "But you can carry lunch."

The girl wrapped both arms around it. "What is it?"

"Sandwiches from the deli. Turkey and tomato, your favorite."

Dinah grinned.

"And salami with lots of peppers and onions for Mac," Damian added.

"'Bout time too," a gruff voice called from the front lawn. "I'm starving." Mac stuck his head through the hedgerow and winked at Dinah. "So you're the one with the food, little lady?"

She nodded, her face aglow. "Right here."

"You get pickles?"

"And soda and chips." Carrying the supplies, Damian followed his boss and Dinah around to the back porch.

The three sat in their usual spot on the steps. Mac dug into the bag and passed around cellophane-wrapped sandwiches, and Damian broke open the bottles of soda and handed Dinah a stack of napkins. Within a minute, a moustache of mustard spread across her freckled face.

"Is that mine?" He pretended to reach for the sandwich she held, but Dinah jumped to her feet and dashed down the steps and around the side of the house. At the corner she stopped, one eye on her brother, and ate the rest of her sandwich through giggles.

"Damn, she's cute," Mac said around a mouthful of pickle.

Damian nodded.

"How's your mom?"

"Pretty good."

"She working?"

"She did the books for a place in Silver Valley, few months back. Didn't work out."

Mac stood, one hand massaging his left knee.

"You all right?"

"Huh?" Mac grimaced. "Oh, yeah. Too many tackles in high school. Left me with no cartilage in either knee. Course I didn't care back then. Told coach to wrap me up, and I'd play 'til I couldn't move."

"And now you really can't."

Mac laughed. "Hell, who thinks about that when you're in high school?"

Damian scanned the lawn. "Where's Dinah?" He didn't like it when she disappeared, even for a few minutes. Made him nervous to have her out of his sight. He supposed it wasn't really fair to his sister, watching over her shoulder all the time, calling her back and interrupting her games of make-believe, but he couldn't help it. He knew what T.J. was capable of.

Mac hobbled down the steps and looked around. After a minute, he pointed to a grove of small pine trees. "Over there."

Damian shaded his eyes and saw the tiny figure. She waved her hands and talked to a chipmunk that sat on the ground beside her. He let out a tense breath. *So quiet. Too quiet.* Sometimes he wished she'd just run screaming in circles. Even on the soccer field, Dinah stood apart from the others, a silent statue who waited for the ball but never slapped her teammates in high fives or cried out when she twisted an ankle. He supposed she'd learned the silence from their mother. He didn't like the idea.

"Hello?" The voice came from somewhere around the front of the house.

Mac looked up at Damian and winked. "Back here, Summer!"

Damian ignored his buddy's knowing glance and leaned against the railing as she approached. Part of him wanted to disappear inside the house. The other part wanted to pick up where they'd left off the other night, after the kiss and before the anger. He cleared his throat and ran one hand along the banister. She looked as good as he remembered. Better, even. One strap of her green tank top had slipped off her shoulder, and he stuck his hands in his back pockets to resist the urge to slide it up again. Or down.

"Hi there."

Summer fixed the strap herself, juggling two white Styrofoam containers. "I brought some goodies." She met his gaze. "Peace offering."

You can't buy me off with brownies, he wanted to say, but the comment made him sound like an ass even inside his own head. *Get over it. Not her fault she's gotta sell the place.*

Mac had crossed to her before the words were out of her

mouth. "Lanie's? All right." He dug into one container and came out with an enormous chocolate chip cookie. "Thanks," he mumbled. The crumbs fell from his mouth.

She offered the other one to Damian, and when he took it, he let his fingers brush against hers. "Thanks."

"I'm sorry," she said under her breath, and Damian's throat closed. God, she had bottomless eyes. Fifty different emotions shimmered under their surface, and for an instant he wanted to lose himself there, just plummet down into her invisible ocean and find a place to float.

She stepped back after a long moment of silence. "Wow." She leaned back. "It looks good. I didn't get a chance to see the roof the other day."

"Sure you want to sell it?" He hated himself for asking, but he had to try. So much lay at stake if they had to pull up roots again.

Her glance skittered away. "What choice do I have?"

"You could subdivide it. You talk to Sadie about that? Maybe we could work something out. I could buy the piece with the farmhouse on it, and..." He'd stayed up thinking about it last night, trying to work out the finances in his head. It was the best solution so far.

She looked away, across the tree line. "I did."

"And?"

"Damian, it would take weeks. Months, maybe. I'd need an engineer. Someone to draw up new blueprints. Someone else to do an environmental study."

He stared at her. "So it's not worth it."

"That's not what I'm saying."

"Maybe not exactly. But it's too much work for you, and—"

"And I don't have that kind of time or money." Her voice

81

shook with emotion. "Believe it or not, I'm not doing this to try and ruin your family."

"You don't know my family. Or anything about me."

Her eyes blazed. "Goes both ways."

"I know that half the reason you're running back to San Francisco so fast is because your father told you—"

"Be very careful what you say next." Her voice, low and threatening, seared him straight through the gut.

He lifted both hands and backed away. "Fine. Let's just make a deal not to talk the rest of the time you're here."

"Fine."

"You have any kind of paperwork for me, put it in the mail. Or give it to Mac."

He thought he saw tears rise in her eyes, but he turned away before he could see for sure.

"Damian—"

"I have things to do." He headed for the nearest scaffolding. Hand over hand, he hauled himself twenty feet into the air. Without a look behind, he pounded nails into shingles until anger and fatigue drove thoughts of Summer Thompson, and that damn green strap sliding down her shoulder, from his mind.

Summer stood in the middle of the lawn, stunned. She'd brought them cookies. She'd apologized and tried to explain herself. And Damian had thrown her words back in her face and then ignored her. If he'd slapped her, it might have hurt less.

Well, fine. I won't bother talking to you again, that's for damn sure. She dusted crumbs from her hands and turned to go. But then she saw a little girl sitting under the trees a few yards away. "Hey, who's that? Mac?"

The stocky man adjusted his tool belt. "Ah, that's Damian's little sister. Dinah. She hangs around here sometimes."

Dinah? Summer glanced up to where Damian worked above them. The one he'd mentioned the other day. The one she'd thought was his girlfriend, his fiancée even. Not his sister. She glared at his back.

"I don't know your family, huh?"

Summer strode across the lawn, watching Dinah sing and trace patterns in the grass as she approached. The girl's hands moved in circles, fingers fluttering. In her lap lay a pile of daisies and dandelions. She seemed to be enjoying herself, but she didn't smile. Rather, a serious look darkened her face, making the expression in her eyes appear much older than the seven or eight years old Summer guessed she probably was.

"Hi there." Summer knelt beside her. "I'm Summer Thompson."

Dinah didn't say anything for a minute. Her hands continued to orbit an imaginary sun above the grass, skimming the surface in rhythm to her humming. Finally she raised her head. "Hi."

"What are you playing?"

Dinah placed her hands on her knees and looked at her lap. "Just a game I made up."

"What's it called?"

The little girl exhaled at the question, and Summer recalled how she herself had been as a child, impatient of adults who tried to understand her language or pretend they remembered what it was like to be young and alone.

"It doesn't have a name."

Summer leaned back on her heels. *She's carrying around*

the weight of the world with the emotions of someone twenty years older. Why?

"Are you going to make us leave our house?" Dinah looked up from her game. "Damian said some lady was going to sell it and make us leave."

Guilt stabbed Summer in the chest. "Oh, sweetie. No, I'm not. Not if I can help it." *Terrific.* Now she'd just lied to a little girl. She thought a minute. "Hey, have you seen the inside of this house? The one your brother is working on?"

Dinah shook her head, but curiosity filled her wide brown eyes.

"Would you like to?"

"Okay."

Summer stood and held out a hand. The girl pushed herself to her feet but didn't take it, and she kept her distance as they walked back to the house. Summer put her hand in her pocket instead and watched the girl's thin back and long legs move in silence. Something about the way Dinah carried herself, the shift of her shoulders and the jut of her chin, reminded her of Damian. An old, familiar ache pulsed inside her—the wish for a sibling still living. The wish for two parents or a close-knit family like the Hunters'. Funny how a few days back in Pine Point could set those old bruises to hurting.

A cell phone rang as she and Dinah neared the house. Summer checked her pocket, but she'd left her own in the car.

Two stories up, Damian answered his. "Mom? What's wrong?"

The concern—no, the almost-fear—in his voice jerked her attention upward. Damian stuck his hammer in his tool belt and was on the ground in less than ten seconds. A combination of panic and anger contorted his expression. "Slow down. Dinah's right here, with me. Of course I'm sure. I'm looking at her." He wrapped an arm around his sister and drew her close.

"Did you call the police? Well, call them right now. Did you lock the doors? Did you get the number off Caller ID? I'll be right there." He dropped the phone into his pocket. Without looking at Mac, he yelled up, "Gotta take Dinah home and check on my mom, okay? I'll be right back."

From the balcony, Mac grunted assent.

Damian pulled off his tool belt and ran a rag across his forehead.

"Everything all right?" Summer asked, though clearly it wasn't.

He didn't answer.

Dinah's lip trembled. "Is Mom okay?"

Her brother smiled, but a muscle in his jaw twitched. "She's fine. She just got a phone call that made her nervous, so we're going home to make sure she feels safe." He took his sister by the hand and led her toward the path that wound around the property to the farmhouse. Urgency hovered over them, a cloud of tension that grayed the day. In another moment, they were gone.

Summer shaded her eyes. "Hey, Mac?"

"Yeah?"

"What was that all about?"

He leaned both arms on the balcony railing. "Not sure. Damian's mom has an ex who's bad news. I know they moved here to get away from him, but...maybe he's back in the picture."

Summer's shoulders sagged as the guilt around her heart deepened. "Really?"

Mac nodded. "He keeps telling his mom to get a restraining order, but I guess she hasn't yet."

She shivered. No wonder Dinah walked around scared of her shadow; no wonder Damian kept one eye on home. *You can't read this place. Closed doors hide so much.*

Summer made her way back to her car, turning over possibilities inside her head. Maybe she could work something out with Sadie or an engineer after all. She couldn't turn the Knights out of their house, not if some crazy ex-husband was stalking them. If they'd found safety here in Pine Point, why should she rip that away from them? Dinah's solemn face appeared in her mind's eye, and her heart broke a little. She knew enough about ghosts to know they never stopped haunting you.

She stared at the mountains. Why couldn't the lives people built here match the idyllic hills or the green lawns that formed such perfect patchworks when seen from the highway? Why did shadows always have to carve things up into an ugly, fractured mosaic? Why did pain always ride on the heels of happiness?

And why the hell did she care so much about someone she'd met less than a week ago?

Chapter Eight

"Mom?" Damian fumbled with his key and rushed into the house.

"In here." The voice came from her bedroom. He crossed the hall and pushed open the door.

Hannah sat on the bed, facing him. Though white, her face remained composed, with her hands folded in her lap like small, fragile birds.

"Are you okay?" Damian wrapped his arms around her and pulled her close. Dinah stood in the doorway, brows knit together and tears in her eyes.

"I'm fine." Hannah's gaze flickered toward her daughter and she lowered her voice. "I called the police. They're going to file a report."

"Did they trace the number?"

"They said they couldn't. It was a pre-paid cell phone or something." She sighed and turned away from him. "He called my cell phone, Damian, not the house. That's a good thing. He doesn't know where we are."

But how long until he finds out? Damian's hands tightened into fists. "What about a restraining order?"

"He isn't here. He's probably a thousand miles away, just making noise."

"You don't know that. He could be hiding out in the next town over." Damian's knuckles turned white as his anger grew. "File one anyway. Just in case."

"I don't want to turn it into something uglier than it already is," she said. "I don't want Dinah thinking her father is a monster."

He scowled. She was wrong; T.J. *was* a monster. It didn't matter whether he'd fathered Dinah or not.

She leveled her gaze on him. "Let it be. Please."

"Maybe we should at least get an alarm system or have the police drive by on a regular basis." T.J. already had her cell number. A new address and a couple of deadbolts wouldn't keep that bastard away forever.

Hannah sighed. "I don't know. Maybe." She leaned against the pillows. "I think I'll lie down for a while."

"I'm here if you need anything." He pulled a blanket over her shoulders.

She murmured a response, already half-asleep. Underneath closed lids, blue veins pulsed as she headed toward dreams. Weak sunlight winked through the open blinds, but in a few minutes she breathed the silent, steady rhythm of someone far away, lost in slumber and glad to be there.

Damian eased the door shut. Behind him, Dinah waited in the hallway. He ran a hand over her ponytail and felt his heart tremble. Why couldn't they live a normal life in Pine Point like everyone else? Why did the past have to rear up in their faces? He squared his shoulders. No matter what, he'd protect Dinah and Hannah. *No matter what.*

"Want something to drink?" He didn't have to go back to the jobsite right away. Mac would understand.

Dinah stared at him with her lips pressed into a straight,

silent line. "Okay." Her quiet understanding broke his heart. They headed for the back porch and sat side-by-side, sipping glasses of iced tea and watching the light change.

"That lady at the house..." Dinah began.

Damian found some mosquitoes to slap. "Summer Thompson."

"I know her name," Dinah said with impatience, and Damian forgot that she'd talked with Summer under the trees. "Is she going to make us leave?"

His chest tightened. "I don't know. I hope not." How he wished he could comfort her, tell her something else. His cell phone rang and he jumped. He checked the screen but didn't recognize the number that came up. *Call this number, you bastard. I dare you. I'll have you arrested within the hour.* But it wasn't T.J.

"Hi, Damian." Joyce Hadley's soprano tones bubbled across the line.

"Oh. Hey." He studied the pattern of the sunlight on the floor.

"How's Dinah? All ready for her big game this weekend?"

"Yeah, I guess. What's up?" Maybe he owed money for Dinah's uniform or was supposed to organize the parents' carpool next week.

"Well..." She drew out the syllable in anticipation, as if she were about to announce the grand prize of a game show. "My parents are having a bunch of people over for a party on the lake next weekend. Wondered if you could make it."

This is a social call? Damian closed his eyes. *No way. Not on your life.*

"You can bring Dinah if you want," she added.

He reconsidered for a half-second and then shook his head.

Sweetening the deal by inviting his kid sister wasn't enough to sway him. "Sorry. Mac and I have to work straight through the weekends. No time off during building season." He tried to sound flip, as if he wasn't turning down her so much as the notion of partying in general.

For a minute she didn't say anything, and he wondered if the lie rang as hollow on her end of the line as it did on his. "Yeah, well, it's okay. I know you're busy," she said. "Let me know if you change your mind."

Damian closed the phone and shoved it back into his pocket. He wondered if he'd said the wrong thing. Any guy in town would give fifty bucks to be in his place. Joyce Hadley had been after him for months. Why the hell didn't he just go out with her? He laced both hands behind his head and stared out the window as the answer crawled up from his heart. *Because I feel nothing when I look at her.* He tried to picture himself kissing Joyce, winding that long hair around his fingers, breathing her in. It didn't work. Instead he saw a painted pink mouth and painted pink nails, a tinny laugh and shallow eyes. As much as he sometimes hated himself for it, he'd never been able to date simply for the sake of dating. He needed more—a soul to burn for, someone to open up the darkest corners of his mind and heart and make him laugh from the inside out. A sharp pain stabbed him in the chest. He'd felt that way once, a long time ago. But something like that didn't happen twice in a lifetime.

Did it?

Chapter Nine

"Gabe, you want lunch? I'm doing a deli run." One of the part-time medics stuck his head into the break room of the Adirondack Region Ambulance Corps.

Gabe glanced up from the reports on his desk. "Sure. Gimme a foot-long Italian. Extra pickles on the side too." He fished out a ten and passed it to the newbie, who was stuck with lunch patrol this week.

"You got it."

"Thanks." Gabe scrawled a signature across the last report and slid them all into a folder. Quiet morning, which was good for the EMTs on duty, but not so good for the thoughts rattling around inside his head. He reached for the remote and flipped on the TV in the corner. At eleven in the morning, it looked like his choices were bad talk shows or cartoon reruns. He left the station on Bugs Bunny laughing at Elmer Fudd and turned up the volume. Closing his eyes, he rolled his head from side to side. He tried to believe that seeing Summer Thompson yesterday didn't have anything to do with last night's lack of sleep or the tension now squeezing his neck in two. He wanted to call her. He didn't want to call her. He had no idea what he'd say if he saw her again.

He changed the channel and tried to listen to a weepy teen tell the father of her baby she wanted him back.

The distraction didn't work. All he saw was Summer's face. That night. The accident and everything that happened after. *Does she know?* He slid open a drawer in the desk he shared with two other guys. A small blue ball lay inside, and he pulled it out. Hand to hand, back and forth, he tossed it in higher and higher arcs.

"Gabe, I'll need you to stand over here." Chief Walters' *double chin bobbed as he spoke. "Been drinking tonight, son?"*

Gabe shook his head and chewed furiously on a stick of gum. "No, sir."

"Mm hmm. Then you won't mind blowing into this for me, will you...?"

"Shit." Gabe squeezed the ball between his fingers until he thought it might split in two. He hadn't thought about that night in years. He'd done his time, come back home and tried to convince Pine Point he wasn't a bad guy. Some people in town believed him. Some didn't. Of course, most people didn't know what had really happened the night Donnie Thompson died, and Gabe wasn't sure it was his place to tell them. He'd gone about his own business, slipped on the skin of a paramedic and blended back into his hometown the best he could. The job came easy, and he liked it most days, which wasn't really a surprise. Rescuing made sense to him. It always had.

His fingers drummed the desk. Today's early humidity had sunk into his knees, and they ached more than they had in a long time. Or maybe it wasn't the humidity at all.

"Fuck it."

He yanked his cell phone from his pocket and dialed the number for Point Place Inn. Didn't matter that it had been almost ten years. Didn't matter that they hadn't spoken or touched since that night under the stars. Some things, good or bad, just tied you to another person forever.

"Please read over this plea bargain, Mr. Roberts, and then sign at the bottom indicating your agreement..."

The voicemail in Summer's room picked up, and Gabe left a message. She was leaving in a few days, that much he knew. Whether she'd return his call or agree to have a meal with him, he could only guess. He turned up the volume and threw the ball across the room, where it hit the wall just beside the TV. His headache grew.

The funeral. The sentencing. The nightmares. He glanced outside at the cars that drove down Main Street and the mothers who pushed their babies in strollers under the morning sun. For a moment, he imagined he could see her in the distance. He retrieved the ball, laid it back in the drawer and ran a hand over his forehead, slick with perspiration.

They needed to talk. From what he'd heard around town, Ron Thompson had sent his daughter to Chicago two days after the accident without telling her anything except that he didn't want her to come back to Pine Point. Gabe grimaced. Not fair, the ghosts and the questions she must have been living with all this time. She needed to know things about the accident her father had never told her. Yeah, Summer Thompson deserved that much.

CR80

"Oh, Summer, it's gorgeous," Sadie Rogers gushed. In her yellow poly-cotton blend suit, the wide-hipped woman stood in the middle of the kitchen and waved a pen. "You could get much more than you're thinking of asking. With this space and all the bedrooms upstairs, and the rental property out back..." She trailed off and scribbled something on her legal pad. Dots of mascara had fallen onto her cheeks, and her blouse had dampened at the collar. A good forty pounds heavier than back in high school, Sadie breathed heavily as she pushed curls off her forehead. A few gray hairs sprinkled her hairline.

"I just—I wanted to ask you about changing the listing." Summer took a deep breath. *This will change things. This decision—it will slow everything down.* "I want to leave the rental house as a contingency. I want the Knights to be able to stay after it's sold."

Sadie stopped writing and clicked her ballpoint pen. "Oh, but—"

"I know what you said. I still want to do it."

"You're sure? I think it'll be harder to find a buyer..."

"But not impossible."

"No. Of course not. It'll just take the right person."

Summer nodded. "That's okay, then." Wasn't everyone looking for the right person to do something? Her cell phone buzzed in her pocket, but she ignored it.

"Well, okay, then. If you're absolutely sure." Sadie stuck her notepad into her enormous purse and tiptoed toward the back door in her three-inch heels. "I'll have to draw up a new contract." She struggled to pull a thick leather calendar from her purse. "I can have this ready for you tomorrow morning." She wet one finger and flipped the calendar pages. Post-it notes stuck out in all directions like blue and yellow flowers. "Is nine-thirty okay? The twins have swimming lessons at eight."

"That's fine."

Sadie scribbled something on a new Post-it and attached it

to the page. "I thought you were leaving soon."

So did I. "I'll change my flight. Not a big deal to stay a few more days." Yeah, like that wasn't the biggest lie she'd told herself all week.

Summer crossed her fingers behind her back and hoped that a few more days in Pine Point wouldn't be any better or any worse. She could keep the flashbacks at bay for a little longer. She could avoid Gabe and everything that churned up memories of her life here a decade ago. Couldn't she?

CS&SO

As soon as Summer stepped inside Dolly's Diner, Joe Bernstein waved a lanky arm from a corner booth. "There you are."

"I'm late. Sorry." She planted a kiss on the wrinkled cheek and slid into the seat opposite him.

"What can I getcha?" Margaret, the middle-aged waitress who had worked at Dolly's as long as Summer could remember, sidled up from behind the counter. A large wad of gum moved around her mouth, and she jotted down their order with a stubby pencil that appeared from a thick reddish bun atop her head.

"So how's work?" Summer asked after they placed their orders.

Joe smiled. "Ah, the office is fine."

"But?"

"But I've decided that this will be my last semester teaching at the college."

"You're kidding." She rolled her straw wrapper into a tiny ball. "I thought you loved working there." The ball worked its way between her fingers, back and forth.

"I do. But I'm getting old, and—"

"Please. You're barely sixty."

"I'm getting old enough that I'd like to do other things with my life than convince young adults why they should care about ancient history."

Summer flicked the paper ball into the ashtray and looked up. "Of course they should care! We can't understand where we are, and who we are, unless we know where we've come from."

He chuckled.

"Why are you laughing? It's true."

"Of course it's true. I'm laughing because you sound like me thirty years ago, full of fire and ready to wrestle with anyone who couldn't understand why studying the Civil War or the California Gold Rush was of any importance."

"But you're the reason I love it so much." All the nights at her kitchen table, flipping cards with her father, Joe had woven story upon story of long-gone civilizations, of wars fought for love and money and power, as Summer sat beside them and listened with fascination. "You made it matter."

He smiled. "You flatter me. But it's time for me to go." He raised a hand when she opened her mouth to protest again. "I can't stay up past eight o'clock and they always give me those god-awful night classes that go until ten. They'll hire someone else, someone younger. It's only two classes a semester, anyway."

"It won't be the same."

"Well, I'd like to think I'll be tough to replace. Don't know as that's the case, though."

Margaret delivered two cups of coffee, and Joe fumbled with the chipped plastic box of sugar packets. "Still leaving town so soon?"

Summer didn't answer for a moment. She wasn't sure how to explain the thoughts that had consumed her for the last three hours. "I'm not sure." She sighed. "Actually, I have to change my flight."

"Really? Why?"

"I decided to sell the house with a rental contingency, which is gonna take a little longer to work out. I don't want to evict the Knights."

"That's rather kind of you."

"I'd like to think I'm a kind person once in a while."

He took a long sip of coffee. "Ever think about keeping the place for yourself?"

One corner of her mouth twitched. *Second person to ask me that in less than a day.* "No. Why would I?"

"You have friends here. A past. It's the place where you grew up."

She shook her head. "I don't care. That—it's all gone." Her chest tightened. "My father told me never to come back, Joe. He made that clear the day I left." And the two times she'd spoken to him on the phone years later.

"He had a hard time dealing with your brother's death."

"And I didn't?" Her voice broke.

"He thought it would be better for you someplace else. Easier."

She shook her head. "I don't think that's it. I think he hated knowing I was alive and Donnie wasn't." She pressed her fingertips to her mouth. "So why the hell leave me a house here? I still don't get it. It's almost like..." She stopped. *Like he wanted to make me pay. Like he wanted to make me suffer after all.*

97

Joe drummed his fingers on the table. "Maybe it isn't exactly what you think. Maybe he was trying to—"

"Make peace? Apologize for throwing me away like I didn't matter?" She drew in a deep breath. "More like he wanted to drag me back here and remind me what I did. How Donnie dying was my fault..." Her eyes filled.

Joe set his mug on the table hard enough that coffee sloshed over the side. "Your brother's death was not your fault."

"You don't know that." Summer reached for a napkin and blew her nose. No one did except Gabe Roberts. No one else had been there that night. No one else could bring back the memories that her own brain had tucked away for good. A stone pressed down on her chest, and she tried to find a normal rhythm to her breath. She couldn't. Instead, the tears came harder. A couple sitting at the next table glanced over but she didn't care. She didn't recognize them anyway. Tears flowed between her fingers and down her wrists.

"What's this really about? Your brother? The house? Or something else?"

Joe's voice sounded far away and Summer fought against the dots that swirled at the edges of her peripheral vision. One hand gripped the table so tightly she thought she might break off a piece of Formica. "I can't remember," she whispered.

Joe's face, at the end of a long tunnel, leaned closer. "Remember what?"

"Summer, look at me. If anyone asks, this is what you have to say..."

She tried to nod and agree. But her head ached, and she couldn't pay attention to Gabe, even though he held her quivering chin in one hand and stared straight into her eyes as he spoke. His words didn't make any sense, anyway. They were mixed up, backwards, not the truth at all.

Summer tried to focus on the lawyer's craggy face. More flashbacks. They came more frequently now, almost every few hours. And yet—

"I can't remember what happened that night."

Joe blinked, and for a long time he said nothing. Margaret delivered their sandwiches, greasy Reubens with greasier fries on the side. Joe harrumphed, and his mouth twitched a little. Summer realized after a moment that he was trying to figure out how to shape his next words in just the right way.

"I think you're very lucky that time, or pain, or a combination of both, has blocked out the accident."

"No." She shook her head. That might have worked for the last ten years. But now that she was back... "I want to remember," she whispered. "I need to know."

Why the urge had gripped her so tightly in the last forty-eight hours, she had no idea. Maybe it was the memories leaking through the veil of consciousness more and more since she'd set foot on the East Coast. Maybe it was seeing the spires of the cemetery gate rising out of the trees behind the damn house. Or maybe it was a combination of all of the above, along with being thrust back into her past without realizing she was missing so many of the pieces that made it up.

"Tell me," she said.

He laid a hand on hers. "You don't need to hear it."

"Please."

He sighed. "I don't know much, really." He stopped until she squeezed his hand to urge him on. "You and Gabe had taken Donnie to the drive-in the night after graduation."

"He wanted to see the new Bruce Willis movie," she

murmured. "Donnie thought Gabe was the coolest guy on the planet." *So did I.*

"It was eleven-thirty or so, and you were all headed home, far as anyone can tell."

She nodded. *We were going to drop Donnie off with Dad and then go back to Gabe's lake house...*

"Mamie and Herb Talbot were on their way home from visiting their grandkids over in Silver Valley. Got to you a few minutes after it happened and called it in."

"I don't remember that. Or them."

"Probably in shock already." Joe spread his hands wide on the table; gnarled knuckles and graying sprouts of hair stuck up from each finger. "You and Gabe were out of the car by the time they got there, banged up but okay." His brows drew together. "Cops couldn't figure out why you both got out so fast, but then..."

She pressed her fingers against his. "But then what?"

He blinked. "You were looking for Donnie, of course. He was thrown from the car."

"Wait—what?" Summer closed her eyes. *I didn't know where Donnie was. I thought he was in the backseat.* "He wasn't wearing his seatbelt?"

Joe shook his head. "He didn't survive the crash." He said the words quickly.

But that wasn't true. "I heard Donnie talking, calling for me, after we were hit."

Joe frowned. "I don't know if that's possible. Maybe."

Summer didn't speak, though she'd just realized something else. She and Gabe hadn't gotten out of the car to look for Donnie. She would put her hand on a Bible and swear to that. They both thought he was still strapped into the backseat. Then why? Bleeding and dizzy, why on earth would they have unstrapped their seatbelts and crawled out of a twisted piece of metal?

"Summer, get out of the car. Now." Gabe pulled at her arm, hard.

"I can't." Things hurt, like her head and her left arm. And her ankle.

"Yes, you can." The seatbelt snapped free from her shoulder. "Come on." He dragged her across the seat and out the open door.

Did he think the car was going to explode? Then why not pull Donnie out too? There'd been no smell of gas, no smoke that she remembered. Summer grabbed at it, a murky reason that swam at the very edge of her memory. *There was something wrong that night.* She tried again to recall it. She and Gabe had taken Donnie out before. As long as they were home before midnight, her father didn't care. Gabe was the best driver she knew. He never sped or took turns too fast, not with her or Donnie in the car. That was part of the reason she hadn't fought too hard when her father made her wait to get her junior license. She'd rather be with Gabe, going anywhere at all, than driving herself down a road that led in circles.

Joe picked up his sandwich. "You had a sprained ankle and some bad cuts from hitting the windshield. Nothing too serious. But then you went into shock as soon as they got you to the hospital. They kept you a couple days, for observation." He paused. "And Gabe—"

"Where is he buried?"

Joe wiped his mouth. "Sorry?"

"My brother. Do you know where his grave is?"

"Ah, yes. Of course." And he told her, right down to the last detail about the funny tufts of grass and the spread of wildflowers that grew under the biggest oak tree in the town's cemetery.

ᘒᘔ

The road curved away from town and became more overgrown the farther in she drove. Pine trees arched down toward her car and blocked the sun. They scraped their branches along her windows. A dust cloud rose up behind her.

By the time Summer parked in front of All Saints' solid black gates, clouds had gathered and turned the whole afternoon gloomy. Thunder rumbled as she opened the door and tested the ground. Good thing she'd worn sensible running shoes today rather than designer heels. She picked her way across the rutted road and stopped under the curved wrought iron letters. Her chest tightened.

"Miss Thompson, can you tell us who was driving the car?" Chief Walters put one hand on her shoulder. She stared at a mangled piece of metal at her feet. It looked like it might have been a mirror, or part of a door panel ripped away in the impact. Her head hurt.

"Summer?"

She looked up. Above them a solitary stoplight blinked, red one way, yellow the other. Of course she knew who'd been driving. What kind of a question was that? She looked past the police chief at the bleary-eyed man who stumbled on the side of the road. Blood dripped from a cut on his head and from his mouth.

"Mr. Hartwell," she whispered. In a breath, she indicted the elementary school custodian.

The policeman nodded and closed his notebook.

Summer forced herself to step through the gate and ignore the wave of dizziness that swept over her. *Follow the path on the right,* Joe had told her. *It goes all the way to the back. Big oak tree standing in the northeast corner. Can't miss it. Donnie's buried right underneath.*

It took her less than a minute to find it.

She drew in a breath and dropped to her knees. A simple stone with simple printing rose a few inches off the ground. She pulled at the weeds that choked the letters of his name. *Donald Francis Thompson. Beloved Son. Bright Angel. Forever Missed.*

Here at the back of the cemetery, she heard nothing at all except a whisper of wind through the trees. She glanced at the stones around her and saw familiar names: Hadley, Simpson, Graves, Bernstein. A few hundred yards away, wilting flowers surrounded a new swell of ground. She leaned over and laid her cheek on the plain white marker. As she knelt there, unmoving, the sun came out again. Eyes closed, she felt its warmth on one side of her face, a granite chill on the other.

"I miss you."

Donnie's stone didn't say *beloved brother,* and yet he'd been just that. The tagalong, the brat, the grass-stained kid who caught snakes and hid them in her closet. The baseball player. The country music lover. The round-eyed face that listened to her problems, the little boy who brought her breakfast in bed every year on her birthday.

One week past thirteen, he'd left her. Summer let her fingers trace the letters and dig into the edges that had worn smooth with time and wind. At twenty-eight she'd lived more

103

than two whole lives to Donnie's one. Nothing seemed more unfair.

She sat back on her heels. At least her father had picked a good spot, quiet and private—though what corner of a cemetery wasn't, when you thought about it? It overlooked the sloping hill that led down to a stream a hundred yards below. Not a bad place, if you had to choose. Of course, Ronald Thompson shouldn't have had to. His son shouldn't have been in the ground at all; he should have been finishing college, starting a job, bringing home a girl, sketching out a life.

Summer rocked to a stand and glanced over her shoulder. Above the trees rose the top of the mansion. She recognized the outline and the way three stories speared the clouds. She couldn't hear anything, and yet she knew Mac and Damian were working less than a mile away from where she stood.

Something inside her chest thawed. *I can see it from here.* She pushed her hair behind her ears and realized for the first time that maybe her father hadn't just bought the house so he could stand at the top of the second floor landing and see the ground that held his dead son. Maybe he'd bought it so that someone standing in this open grassy area could look up and catch the glimpse of a familiar silhouette in one of the windows. Or so that someone sleeping here could sense that family lived and breathed and loved just a few hundred yards away. Maybe that kind of connection went both ways.

She scanned the cemetery. The bouquet of bright red tulips she'd brought with her looked silly, out of place in a daisy-and-dandelion-filled meadow. Again she studied the rooftop of the house in the distance. She raised the flowers to her nose and breathed in the heavy, heady scent.

So many questions. So many pieces that didn't fit the puzzle inside her head. Summer blinked with a sudden realization. She wasn't going to change her flight just so she could find a way for the Knights to stay in their farmhouse a little longer.

She was going to change her flight because she couldn't leave Pine Point until she knew exactly what had happened the night her brother died.

Chapter Ten

Summer and Gabe sat in a shadowy corner of Marc's Grille. Around them, plush chairs and elegant place settings waited for the dinner crowd to arrive. She shifted and adjusted her blue silk sundress. Legs crossed at the ankles, she tucked her Jimmy Choos under the table. She pulled a dinner roll in half and separated it into smaller and smaller pieces without eating it. Crumbs fell onto her plate as she looked past Gabe, through the restaurant's enormous front window. Outside stretched a quarter-mile block of spotless storefronts, manicured landscaping and wrought-iron benches. Posh boutiques and cozy bars had replaced the rambling cornfields of her childhood. This new avenue, Park Place Run, looked like it had been lifted from the east side of some upscale city and transplanted amid the hills and farmland.

"I won't bite," Gabe said.

Summer looked back at him and felt herself color. "Sorry." She couldn't meet his gaze so she steadied herself on the cleft in his chin. "It's just—it's been a long day." That was the truth, anyway. *Why did I agree to this? What are we doing here?*

The front door opened, and Summer recognized the couple who entered. She smiled and waved. The young woman took a step toward their table and then stopped. With a tight smile, she laced her fingers through her husband's and pulled him toward the hostess stand instead.

"That was weird."

"What?"

"Alyssa Reynolds. Or Williams now, I guess. Didn't you play ball with the guy she married? Frank?"

"Yeah." Gabe dug into his salad.

"She just totally ignored me."

"Don't worry about it."

"But—"

"You know how people are here."

"They used to be nice."

"They still are nice. They just keep to themselves."

"But she didn't even say hello." Surely Alyssa remembered her. They'd sung together in the school choir for three years.

"Maybe she's not sure what to say to you." He met her gaze. "People might feel a little awkward."

"I guess." Summer pushed lettuce leaves around her plate. "This is a great place," she said after a minute.

"It is." Gabe set down his fork and studied her. "The owner worked hard to get it going."

Conversation lapsed into silence. She had so many questions she wanted to ask and no idea where to begin. The waitress came and cleared their salad plates. An open bottle of wine sat on the table between them. Gabe split it between their glasses and sent it away with the woman, empty.

The front door opened again and this time elderly Grant Knicke walked in. The former elementary school principal held hands with a little girl decked out in a ballerina's tutu, leotard and princess crown. A slender woman followed them, carrying a toddler on her shoulders.

"Oh, there's Mr. Knicke. And Mandy and her kids." Summer smiled at the man beloved by every kid in Pine Point. With a stash of lollipops in his desk drawer, Mr. Knicke had been head of the only school in town where kids actually tried to get into trouble, just so they could spend ten minutes in the spacious corner office with the gentle giant who let you cry into his handkerchief without calling home or telling your parents.

The man glanced at Summer and she thought she saw recognition in his eyes. She pushed her chair back, meaning to go over and say hello. He nodded in her direction, looked briefly at Gabe and then patted his granddaughter on top of her head and steered her to the other side of the restaurant.

What the hell is going on here? She frowned and tried to shrug off the paranoia. Maybe Gabe was right. Maybe people just didn't know what to say.

When her salmon arrived, she speared it with a fork, glad for the distraction. "So how did you end up working as a paramedic, anyway?"

He sliced his filet mignon. "They needed more guys in the corps. And I always liked medicine—you remember that."

She did.

"Figured it'd be as good a job as any."

She took a long sip of wine. "It never gets to you? Especially after what happened to us?"

He laid down his fork. "That's part of the reason I chose it."

"Oh." Her heart crept into her throat. "Well, you're braver than I am." *Ask him. Ask him what really happened that night.*

He smiled. "Or dumber. Haven't really figured it out yet. How did you get into...whatever it is that you do?"

Summer blew out a long breath. "I'm a curator for a small museum in San Francisco."

"Ah. Yeah, well, you always were a history buff back in school. All those dates and details. You like it?"

"Love it. I get to arrange exhibits, do some research, set up shows and workshops for kids in the local schools..."

"Sounds cool."

"It is." More silence.

She pushed away her fish, mostly uneaten, and leaned back in her chair. "So are you dating anyone?" Her gaze dropped to his left hand. No ring. "Girlfriend? Fiancée?"

He chuckled. "Nah. Playing the field, that's all. No one came close to you."

She let herself smile. "Of course they didn't." A familiar ache rolled around her heart and fell away. "So?"

"So what? The dating thing?" He shrugged. "I, ah, hooked up with Tara Hadley for a while, if you can believe it."

"I can, actually."

"Then she left me for some older guy. She got bored with him, so we started going out again. We'd go out for a few months, break up, get back together a few months later...until about two or three years ago. She went on a trip to Jamaica with her sisters and came back married."

"Married?" Rachael hadn't shared that bit of Hadley gossip with Summer.

Gabe shrugged again. "Lasted about a year. Long enough for the guy to get his green card and dump her. Since then, we don't really talk."

Summer wondered about that. Relationships that wandered through the years rarely ended with neat corners and final goodbyes. Rather, they were messy, with residual feelings and a history that didn't always fade with ease. She knew that better than anyone.

They finished dinner and ordered coffee, full-strength for both of them.

"When did you start drinking the hard stuff?" He'd always hated coffee back in high school, even when all his friends started drinking it mornings after a big game or a bigger party.

"After the accident."

And just like that, the ice broke. The past swerved into the present, and everything came rushing back.

Summer sat without moving while Gabe stared into his coffee. Steam rose into the air. She reached for his hand and he let her take it. "Gabe." She paused. "I wished we'd talked. Said something, or seen each other, or... After it happened, I mean. Before I left."

He stroked his thumb along the ridge of her palm. "Me too."

"Did you—God, this sounds stupid—" She exhaled. "Were you hurt?"

"What do you mean? Physically?"

Or emotionally, or psychologically, or all the other ways something like that can hurt a person. "Yeah." She pulled her hand away again. "Physically."

He dumped two packets of sugar into his coffee. "Just banged up. Bruised back. Broken nose. Nothing too bad." He paused. "You had it worse."

She sipped her coffee and burned her tongue. "I don't remember a lot of what happened. And after—I only know what my father told me, which wasn't much."

He nodded. "I sort of figured."

She opened her mouth to ask him something—*Why did we get out of the car?*—and shut it again. She didn't know how to negotiate this line of questioning, and suddenly she wasn't sure she wanted to hear the answers.

Something beeped.

"Shit." Gabe's hand moved to his lap and he glanced down. "Summer, I've gotta go. I'm on call tonight. Sorry."

She sat back. "Oh. Okay."

Seconds later, the beeper went off again. He pushed back his chair and flagged down the waitress. Outside, a siren wailed down the block.

She reached for her purse. "Let me leave the tip."

"Already got it." Gabe signed the credit card slip and tore off his copy.

"I feel like I owe you."

They moved toward the exit, and the smile she remembered from school flashed across his features. "Oh, you do, Thompson. In ways you can't begin to imagine." He held the door for her and they stepped into a humid evening.

Summer rummaged around in her purse for her car keys. She felt unsettled, as if they'd only just creaked open the past without daring to look inside. She needed more. She wanted more. "Can we maybe have coffee sometime?"

He slid an arm around her waist. "I'd like that." They stood there for a moment without speaking, and then he leaned over and pressed a kiss to her cheek. "How long are you staying?"

"I changed my flight to next week."

"Yeah? Thought you were leaving sooner than that. Any special reason?"

"I'm trying to work out a contingency with the house sale so the renters can stay on." She didn't add that one of the renters had kissed her the other night under moonlight and turned her topsy-turvy with desire. She didn't suppose that was something you confessed to an ex-boyfriend.

An ambulance passed, its lights flashing. Something cold

slipped down her spine, and she marveled again at the fact that Gabe did this, rescued bleeding people the same way they'd been rescued all those years ago. She could never do it. It would be like staying trapped inside that night forever. She shivered.

Gabe caught her gaze and held it longer than he needed to. "It was nice seeing you." His smile faded. "I'm glad you came back. It's good to make peace."

Summer rested in the circle of his arm for another minute. She wasn't sure she had, not yet. She still resented her father. She still missed her brother with a heartache that overwhelmed her. She still wanted to know what had happened that night, under the stars—and only one person could fill in those blanks.

"Coffee sounds good," he said at last.

She nodded.

"I'll call you, then."

She watched him walk away from her without another word, until Gabe Roberts was just a silhouette in the evening and she was left with more questions and more memories and a longing she couldn't explain.

෬෫

Theo eased his battered car into the dirt parking lot. *Bill's*, read the sign above the door. The neon flickered in and out, making it look more like a strip joint in Vegas than the local watering hole it supposedly was. He smoothed both hands over his hair and took his time getting out.

He was close. He could feel it. Screw that private investigator he'd wasted too much money on. After seven hours of driving north from Baltimore, he'd found the junior college Damian had graduated from, and though the bitch in Admissions wouldn't give him any personal info, he had a damn good feeling the kid and his mother were still around. Tracing her cell phone had turned into a dead end, and the number wasn't much good without a location.

Now he was stuck in this piss-ant Adirondack Mountain region trying to blend in and do a little sleuth work without getting noticed. Already had a headache from trying to negotiate the winding roads that connected all these shitty blue-collar towns, and he couldn't find a decent place to get a meal, let alone a beer or two. But he'd found himself a part-time contracting job yesterday, so he could blend in with the locals and do a little spying in the meantime.

Inside, six heads swiveled in unison as he pushed open the door. A ball game played on the television hanging behind the bar, volume off. He lifted his chin in greeting and pulled up a stool.

"Evenin'," said the bartender. His belly hung over a pair of jeans, and arms thick as slabs of meat strained at a faded blue T-shirt.

"Draft," Theo pointed to the tap closest to him. "Thanks."

The rest of the patrons turned back to their game. In the corner, a couple sat holding hands and staring at each other in a way that made Theo want to gag. He trained his gaze on the television.

"You new in town or passing through?" The bartender folded his arms and leaned in.

"Ah, just here part-time, doing some contracting work for a friend." Theo downed half the beer and prayed the guy wouldn't ask him which friend.

"Yeah?" A toothpick shifted from one side of the bartender's mouth to the other. "You working on that new development in Cedar Crest?"

Theo nodded. That, at least, was true.

"Shit. Them houses gonna be mansions. Don't know who the hell can afford 'em."

"Not me, that's for sure."

The bartender guffawed. "Damn straight."

Theo finished his beer and pushed the mug back across the bar. "Another, thanks."

No one spoke for a few minutes. Theo watched the Yankees score two runs against the Cleveland Indians before he got up the nerve to ask the question he really wanted to know. "Hey, anyone know a guy around here name-a Damian Knight?"

The guy closest to him shifted on his stool. Red-eyed, he looked Theo up and down before answering. "Nope." His head turned on a thick neck. "Johnny!"

A man in blue flannel and camo pants looked up from his pool game. "What?"

"Know a guy named Damian Knight?"

The man spit into a cup and shook his head. "Nope. He live in Cedar Crest?"

"Not sure," Theo said carefully. Last thing he needed was to get anyone suspicious. "I worked with him a while back, thought he said something about moving up here. He graduated from Adirondack Community College a few years back."

The bartender leaned over. "Might try Silver Valley or Pine Point, then. Them's the next biggest towns around."

"How far?"

"Silver Valley's just over the mountain. Twenty miles or so. Pine Point's between there and the Thruway. 'Bout an hour from here." He scratched his belly and moved away.

Theo nodded without answering. Easy drive. Maybe he'd try it tomorrow or the next day, see what the places looked like.

The guy beside him was still talking. "Not much to see that

114

way." He burped. "Saratoga Springs, farther up the highway, that's a place worth checking out. Horses, if you're a betting man, or..." He drifted off as the bartender turned up the volume on the TV. A player in pinstripes rounded the bases.

"Not really into the horses, but thanks." Perspiration broke out across Theo's forehead. He grimaced and finished his second beer, tasting the bitter after-flavor of unclean tap pipes.

"'Kay, thanks, 'night," he murmured as he pushed back his stool. The bartender grunted in return. No one else even looked his way.

Outside, pitch black greeted him as soon as the door swung shut. Theo turned around, trying to get his bearings. He could barely make out the treetops and mountain ridges against the ink of the sky. A tiny sliver of moon hung above him, and he tripped finding his way back to the car. Wasn't used to countryside this back-asswards, that was for sure. Not even a damn streetlight out this far. He swore out loud as he tripped again. Fresh anger at his ex-wife mixed with his desire to see her again. She'd deliberately picked a quiet, dark place in which to hide. He knew it. *Suburban Philadelphia wasn't good enough, huh?*

He wondered how Hannah would take to Baltimore because she was damn well coming back there with him. As soon as he found her, he was putting her and Dinah in his car and driving due south. They belonged together, no question about it. He frowned. But if she refused, he'd take Dinah and leave the bitch behind with her smart-ass son. *Damian.* Theo's hands tightened into fists. Last time he'd tried to reason with Hannah, Damian had stepped between them and landed a few lucky punches. Theo would have to take them by surprise or wait for a time when Damian wasn't there at all. He cracked his knuckles. He still had to find Hannah, and he still had to work out a plan, but it was coming together.

"Damn straight," he muttered, echoing the bartender. "Damn straight."

Chapter Eleven

"So I'm thinking of moving into the house." Summer waved away the café's teenage waitress and slurped the last of her piña colada. Despite the umbrella tilted above them, the sun burned down onto the back of her neck.

"What?" Rachael fished a French fry off her plate.

"I met with Sadie this morning, and we decided to list the house with the rental as a contingency. Means the Knights'll get to stay there. But it means I'm staying a few more days too. Gotta get things finalized."

Her friend's voice went up an octave. "You're staying? How long?"

"Another week."

"Wow. Cool."

Summer wasn't sure it was cool at all, but too much nipped at her heels here in Pine Point to turn her back on it a second time.

"You know you could stay at my place, right? I mean, there's an empty bedroom since Cat moved out."

"I know. And I thought about asking you." Summer shrugged. "But I think I'd rather be at the house in case...I don't know. In case Mac and Damian have questions about things. Or in case I do." She wondered how obvious her little white lie was.

"What about the museum? You don't have to rush back?"

"I have great assistants, thank God. And I haven't taken a vacation day in three years. Anyway, the bedroom on the first floor is almost finished, so I thought I'd ask Mac about it. I don't want to keep paying for a motel room if I actually own a house."

"Mm hmm." Rachael lifted two fingers at the waitress and pointed to their empty glasses. She folded her arms on the table. "Now tell me the real reason you're staying. And don't tell me it's because it's gonna take you a week to get all the paperwork settled. You can list a house in two days. And you don't need to be here in town to sell it."

The waitress delivered fresh drinks in frosted glasses, and Summer took a long, deliberate sip.

"Are you staying so you can get back together with Gabe?"

"What? No."

Rachael narrowed her eyes. "Are you sure? I heard you had dinner with him."

"More than sure." She and Gabe had ended things so long ago, there was nothing left between them but a faint buzz, a memory of a place where attraction used to hum. The emotions he'd stirred up at dinner had more to do with sorting through her brother's death than any chemistry left after all this time.

So she was telling herself, anyway.

"I just—" She stopped and tried to think of how to explain. They'd never talked about the accident, she and Rachael. "I'm trying to remember what happened the night my brother died."

Her friend's mouth formed an *O*.

"Since I've been back, I've been having these weird flashbacks. I see parts of the night, parts of what happened. But not the whole thing."

118

"You're kidding."

"The therapist I saw in college told me I probably wouldn't ever remember." She took another sip of piña colada. "So it's weird, now, that I am."

"You have amnesia? All this time?"

"Something like that."

Rachael whistled. "Why didn't you ever tell me?"

"I don't know. Does it make a difference?"

"I guess not." But a funny expression skittered across Rachael's face for a moment. "I'm just surprised, that's all."

Summer lifted her shoulders. "I had dinner with Gabe because I thought maybe he could fill in the blanks. He remembers, I think."

The odd expression came back again. "Yeah, I'm pretty sure he does," Rachael said.

"Why are you looking at me like that?"

Rachael paused. "You don't know what happened to Gabe? After the accident?"

"No. No one ever talked about him. You didn't."

"You never asked."

Rachael's cell phone rang then, and Summer watched a pair of birds chase each other across the sidewalk while her friend made dinner plans with the boyfriend of the month.

"Sorry," Rachael said when she hung up.

"It's fine. What's this guy's name? Seth?"

"Sean. And he's a nice guy, owns a shoe store over in Cedar Crest."

"How long you been seeing him?"

"Three weeks."

"Almost a record, huh?"

"Don't see a ring on your finger either."

"Touché."

They both laughed.

"So what about Damian?" Rachael asked.

"What about him?" Summer felt her cheeks color. She could still taste him inside her mouth, could still feel his hands against the curve of her waist. She wanted to kiss him again. She wanted more than that, actually, and the warmth that grew between her thighs surprised her.

"He's single. He told Cat he's into you. And you just changed your flight so you can stay here." Rachael sucked down half her drink. "If there's nothing left between you and Gabe, then I don't know what you're waiting for. I would have been living on the bare floor of that house three days ago, sawdust and all, just to get a look at Damian first thing in the morning."

Summer laughed. "You're ridiculous."

"Ridiculous, maybe, but with damn good taste." Rachael stuck her sunglasses on top of her head and waved for the bill. "So when do we get you moved in?"

ଊୄ

Damian's Camaro, parked at its crooked angle near the shrubbery, was the first thing Summer saw when she arrived at the house after lunch. She glanced at the rubber-banded stack of papers on the seat beside her.

"Didn't know there was so much to selling a house," she'd said to Sadie that morning.

"It's easier keeping one than selling one," the real estate agent chuckled.

Summer picked up the bag of oatmeal raisin cookies she'd bought and brushed through the hedges. *Well, I'm not keeping it.* That was about the only thing she knew for certain. But that didn't mean she couldn't take advantage of owning it for a few days. Steeling her nerves, she detoured around a pile of paving stones stacked near the front stoop. Talking to Rachael had convinced her, and now she wanted to move in as soon as she could. She just hoped Mac wouldn't laugh when she brought up her bright idea.

"Hello?" She circled the house and looked up. Scaffolding stood against the back balcony and fresh sawdust covered the lawn, but she saw no one. Had they left for a late lunch? She found her way through the kitchen and into the main hallway. Faint banging and grunts sounded somewhere beneath her feet. A minute later the grunts grew louder, coupled with heavy footsteps, and two dust-coated figures emerged from a door at the end of the hall.

"Hey, Summer." Mac raised a hand in greeting. Sneezing, he sprayed a cloud of white into the air. Damian stood behind him and coughed.

"Where were you guys?"

"Basement." Mac waved an arm toward the door behind him. "Supposed to rain later. We wanted to get most of the wood and the sheetrock indoors."

"That's the basement?"

Mac grinned. "Yup. Wouldn't go down there, though. No working lights and plenty of dirt. Probably some rats, too."

"What?"

Damian elbowed his boss. "Don't listen to him. They won't bother you."

"But they're down there?" She eyed the floorboards.

"Maybe one or two," Damian answered. "Nothing to worry about. We put out some traps."

Dust and dirt covered his face and neck, but something in her stomach stirred, and Rachael's words rang in her ears. *I would have been living on the bare floor of that house three days ago, sawdust and all, just to get a look at Damian first thing in the morning.*

"I decided to sell the house with a contingency." Summer said it quickly, before she lost her nerve and he turned away. "Whoever buys it will have to let you stay on and rent for as long as you want."

He stared at her, and his eyes widened. She smiled, and in his gaze she saw herself reflected in the light that illuminated his eyes.

"You did that?"

"Seemed like the right thing to do."

His cheeks colored a little and his voice turned gruff. "Thanks. 'Preciate it."

Summer cleared her throat and held out the white paper bag she'd carried from the car. "I stopped at Lanie's, got the first batch of cookies out of the oven."

Mac had his hands on it before she finished the sentence. "Awesome! Thanks." He reached in and stuffed two into his mouth. Crumbs fell onto his pant legs. Summer laughed. Damian took a couple, then Mac took another and offered her a crumbled one from the bottom, and before she knew it, the bag was empty.

"We're about done here for today," Mac said. "I've got to run over to Silver Valley, pick up a shipment."

"Before you go—"

"Yeah?"

"I—uh—I wanted to ask you...do you think I can move in here?"

Mac frowned. "What do you mean? Into the house?"

"I can't really afford to stay at the motel for another week."

"Oh." Mac folded his beefy arms and considered. "Well, not legally. You're supposed to have a CO."

"A what?"

"Certificate of Occupancy. Piece of paper that means it's safe to live here."

Summer's hopes fell.

"But the building inspector lives in Silver Valley. Doesn't make it over here too often." He winked. "Think it wouldn't be a problem, 'specially if it's just for a few days. I sure as hell won't say anything."

"Really?"

"Sure. We'll get you set up. Suppose we can find you a bed someplace, maybe a dresser or somethin' too, if you need one. Doors are secure enough, and—"

"I'm sure it'll be fine. Nothing much to steal here, anyway."

"Still..." He headed into the kitchen.

"Thanks, Mac." She stole a gaze at Damian, but she couldn't read his face. Mac's mention of a bed had turned her cheeks scarlet, and she thought her best move was to back away until she got herself under control. "Okay, well..." She tucked her purse over her shoulder and turned to leave.

"You don't have to go," Damian said from behind her. She turned around in time to see his cheeks redden too. "I mean, I could use the company, if you want to stick around and check out the room."

Want pooled in her belly. "Okay. Guess I can see what I'm getting myself into." She followed him through the foyer and

123

into the bedroom.

Clouds scudded across the sky. In a matter of seconds the sun vanished and thunder grumbled through thick, heavy air. Damian flipped on a work light near the door and examined the trim along the baseboard.

"This room's great. Huge, too." He hammered and measured as he spoke. When he knelt, the muscles in the backs of his legs flexed, and his hair fell along the sides of his face.

"Everything you guys have done..." Summer tried to look away from him and couldn't. "...it looks great."

He stopped and glanced up at her, knuckling a tape measure. "I really appreciate you letting us stay in the farmhouse."

"Well, Mac told me a little about your mom's ex."

Damian's face darkened. "Yeah."

"Sorry. Didn't mean to bring it up."

"'S alright." He shook his head and drove three nails into the molding. "Thought you were heading back west."

"Trying to get rid of me?" She cocked her head and leaned against the wall, a few feet away from him.

He looked up again. Bright blue eyes took her in and peeled away her outer layer with a single blink. "Nope."

Oh, God. If Damian hadn't been covered with sawdust right then, she would have reached down and touched his mouth, just to feel his lips move against her fingertips.

"I thought maybe—" she began, but a crack of thunder drowned her words. Outside, the sky turned from azure to pitch in a matter of seconds.

"Sorry?" He stood, took a step toward her and closed the distance between them. Two feet. Maybe less. "I didn't hear—"

An instant before thunder drowned out his words, their shoulders brushed, and an electricity ricocheted around the room and landed somewhere close to Summer's knees. The growing breezes tangled the branches; the trees outside appeared and disappeared in erratic rhythm as the wind grew. His breathing quickened. For a moment, there was nothing but silence. Stillness. Hesitation.

Then Damian bent his head and caught her mouth with his. One hand stroked the curve of her chin, and she shivered. His tongue parted her lips, and one arm slipped around her waist. This kiss was stronger than the other night at the lake, more insistent. He pulled her close and lifted her onto her tiptoes. Her hands played over his biceps and she tasted his tongue, something sweet and bitter all at once, like leftover coffee and chocolate and desire. Her nipples tightened, and for a crazy moment she wanted nothing at all between them.

Someone knocked at the front door.

Summer's breath caught in her throat as Damian's hand moved to the swell of her breast. *Please, no,* she willed the unseen visitor. It was probably a deliveryman or Mac with both arms full. *Please go away because I want this man to take me right here, on this floor, with the rain pouring outside and—*

She exhaled as Damian's embrace loosened. He pulled back slightly and after another second dropped both arms and moved away. She stared at him. She tingled in places that hadn't tingled in a long, long time.

The knock came again, louder and longer.

"You expecting someone?" His voice sounded ragged and he kept his eyes on her.

"I don't think so." No one even knew she was here.

"Damian?"

It was a female voice, one that Summer didn't know. The

hair on the back of her neck lifted. She straightened her shirt.

In a heartbeat Damian's face changed and he hurried into the foyer. The front door stood open, with rain and wind blowing inside. A slight, attractive woman hovered on the threshold. With effort, she pulled the heavy door shut.

"What's wrong?" He towered over her in protection.

"Nothing's wrong. I just came by to see the place." The woman turned to Summer and held out a thin, delicate hand. "I'm Damian's mother, Hannah Knight. You must be Summer Thompson."

The funny sense of jealousy that had risen up in Summer's chest vanished. The hood of Hannah's raincoat fell away, and immediately Summer noticed the resemblance between mother and son. Same blue eyes. Same strong jawline. Chiseled features that were beautiful—almost haunting—on her became startlingly attractive on him.

Summer wiped her hands on the back of her shorts and returned the handshake. "Hi, Mrs. Knight. It's so nice to meet you."

"Not Mrs. Just Hannah. Please." She pressed Summer's hands between both of hers. "I ran into Sadie Rogers at the salon a little while ago, and she told me you're letting us stay in the farmhouse." Her eyes filled. "Thank you so much."

"Oh, well...you're welcome." Summer felt embarrassed by the woman's gratitude. She hadn't done much of anything, just put her signature on a couple sheets of paper. "It's really—I wanted to."

Hannah lifted her gaze. She took in the grand foyer, the entrance to the formal front room, the half-open bedroom door. Her eyes widened as she looked at the circular staircase, and she nodded. "It's beautiful. Beyond beautiful, really. I thought it would be, from the outside. When it's all finished, well..."

"It's so big." Summer's gaze moved to Damian, to his hands and his mouth and the way he kept smiling at her. "And it still needs a lot of work."

"Ever thought about keeping it?"

Why did everyone ask her that? Summer shook her head. "I don't think so. It doesn't make much sense. My whole life is out in California now."

"Well, are you going to do any decorating before you go?" Hannah walked into the front room and ran a hand over the chair rail, the wide bay window, the gilt fireplace mantel. "Change the colors, anything like that?"

Damian headed up the stairs as Summer followed the woman and pressed the backs of both hands to her face. His kiss had thrown her off-balance. Again. "I don't know the first thing about any of it. My father bought the house and willed it to me." She stood in front of the bay window and let her gaze rest on the black cemetery gates in the distance. That sobered her. "But I don't live in Pine Point anymore. It would be silly to keep it. He planned most of the major work. I wouldn't even know where to begin with the rest."

Hannah waved a hand. "Ah, read a few magazines, spend an afternoon in a home improvement store, and you'll get plenty of ideas." She looked around. "I'd do this room in pale gray, maybe, or eggshell. Something soft. Redo the window seat, the mantel..." She wandered to the window. "Gorgeous view. Put a couple of chairs here, deep, comfortable ones so you can watch the sunrise—or the stars come out, depending what kind of hours you keep."

Her voice, musical in the stillness, charmed Summer. She stole a glance at Damian's mother and a sudden thought struck her. Hadn't Sadie mentioned something about Hannah working in design before she moved to Pine Point?

"Would you—would you maybe like to help me? Pick out colors, maybe choose some light fixtures or something?" *Might make the place feel a little more like home when potential buyers walk through.* That's what Sadie had told her, anyway. And Summer certainly wanted the sale to happen quickly. Did the request seem ridiculous? She leaned in the doorway. Hannah Knight probably had better things to do with her days than offer color-swatch suggestions to a total stranger.

But the woman's eyes lit up, blue like her son's, bright like her daughter's. "I'd love to. I used to work as an assistant for an interior designer. A long time ago." Her voice rang with an emotion Summer couldn't identify.

"Was that in Poisonwood?"

Hannah looked surprised. "Yes, it was. How did you know?" Before Summer could respond, she answered her own question. "Damian."

Summer nodded. "He mentioned it. Sadie too."

Hannah crossed the foyer and inspected the master bedroom. She smiled as she wandered around the room. "Blues and greens," she said, almost to herself. "I'd do this room in something cozy, relaxing. If you'd like, we could go to Walls and Windows over in Silver Valley to get some ideas. It's a cute design place. Very good prices."

"Okay." Summer looked at her watch. She might not belong in Pine Point for good, but maybe she could find a way to make the next few days a little more interesting. "Tomorrow, maybe? I have some things to take care of this afternoon." She ticked off the list inside her head. Four telephone calls. Three emails. Two press releases and a phone interview with one of the independent papers down in San Diego. *Thank God for telecommunications.*

"I can meet you here at ten, if that works." Hannah

interrupted her thoughts. "Dinah has soccer practice in the morning, but Damian can pick her up and take her to lunch."

"Sounds perfect."

They walked back into the foyer as Damian descended from the second floor. Grinning, he placed a hand on each woman's shoulder. "Someone's talking design down here."

Heat flooded Summer's face.

"You just stick to your hammering and sawing," Hannah said, "and we'll take care of making the place look nice."

He planted a kiss on Hannah's cheek. "Fine by me, Mom." Then he leaned close to Summer. "*Definitely* fine by me," he whispered into her ear, and she shivered.

Summer wondered if he'd kiss her too. He didn't, and then she was glad, because she wasn't sure she'd be able to keep herself from reaching for more.

Chapter Twelve

"Mustard or sage for the small bathroom?" Hannah flipped through a book of paint colors. Behind them, the bells on the door of Windows and Walls tinkled as another customer walked in. Only ten thirty, and already a handful of shoppers filled the tiny shop. Summer recognized a couple of them, but most were strangers.

"I don't know," she sighed, looking back at the thick book. "I'm no good at this."

"Well, then, let's take a couple of each." Within a matter of minutes, Hannah had selected four color samples, plucked two catalogs from the rack in the corner and purchased curtain rod finials in a design Summer would never have chosen but had to admit looked perfect in the sunlight.

They squeezed their way back outside and found a coffee shop down the block.

"Thanks," Summer said. Steaming lattes arrived for both of them. She picked at the edges of an apple fritter. "I really appreciate it."

Hannah smiled. "It's my pleasure. I love color and design, and...making someplace cozy. Took me almost three years, but the farmhouse is almost the way I want it. I've bounced Dinah around so much, I want a place she can call home." She whispered the last word over the edge of her mug.

"Does she take after you that way? With the design, I mean?"

"Well, she's at the age where she thinks pink is the perfect complement for any décor, so it's hard to tell. Maybe she'll grow into it."

"And Damian..." Summer wasn't sure what she meant to say or ask. She just liked the feel of his name on her tongue.

"You know men. They're much better with tools than with fabric swatches. Though sometimes Damian surprises me. He has an eye for detail, for art, that pops out every now and then. I suppose spending most of his life with just his mother has rubbed off." She frowned. "Not in a bad way, I hope."

Summer's brows lifted. She knew enough about family relationships not to prod. She and Hannah had barely met. She had no right to wonder about Damian or his family or how they'd ended up in Pine Point.

The woman sat back in her chair. "Did you know I had Damian when I was just nineteen?"

"Um, no. But wow." Nineteen? Summer could barely remember that year in her own life, the bridge between eighteen and twenty, between the end of her life in Pine Point and the beginning of the rest of it. Just a haze of pain and depression and loss, mostly.

Hannah propped her chin in one hand, and memory tinted her eyes from blue to gray. "I fell in love with the guy working on the apartment house across the street." She smiled at Summer's startled gaze. "Yep. That's where Damian gets his talent. Jimmy was the foreman of the project, the genius. He was better with inside details than the bigger stuff, but he could do anything with his hands." She blushed. "You know what I mean."

Summer smiled. "I do."

"We dated for almost a year before I got pregnant. We were going to get married."

Summer almost didn't want to ask. "He left?"

"He died. Fell off a roof and broke his back. He might have survived, but he was by himself, trying to finish up a job after the other guys had left. No one found him for hours."

"Oh, God. I'm so sorry."

"It was a long time ago." Hannah shook her head. "But I thought I might not even make it through the pregnancy, I cried so much. I was afraid I'd give birth to the saddest child in the world." The emotion in her eyes shifted from sadness to loneliness to resignation and back again. "For a while, I didn't even want to live.

"But you're strong when you're that young." Hannah pulled in a long breath. "You bounce back. And look what I got—a wonderful, handsome, talented son. He changed my life the instant I saw him. I never knew I could love someone so much. So unconditionally." Her face brightened. "He looks so like Jimmy, sometimes I forget when Damian walks in the room that he isn't his father."

Summer tried to imagine a young Hannah and the man she'd fallen in love with. Did he have Damian's quiet confidence? His mannerism of brushing the hair from his face, his smile that crinkled at the corners? Had he waved at Hannah from rooftops with a strong arm and glowed with the perspiration of a job well done? She guessed so, and she wondered at the difficulty of living with an image of the person you'd loved and lost so many years ago.

Dad did that, she thought suddenly. *After Mom died in childbirth. He looked at me every day until I was eighteen.* For the first time she wondered if Donnie's death wasn't the only reason he'd sent her away.

"After Damian was born, I stayed with my mom for awhile. That was when I worked for Flora's Designs." Hannah smiled. "I loved to create a picture in my mind and watch it come to life in a room." She traced the pattern of the glass-topped table. "I worked there until Damian was about twelve or thirteen, and then I met T.J."

"Your ex?"

Hannah nodded. "Also a construction worker." She chuckled, but it wasn't a happy sound. "I guess I have a weakness for them. Our house needed repairs, so Mom and I looked in the yellow pages. Called the least expensive company we could find, and T.J. showed up."

"What was he like?"

The woman shrugged. "Oh, your typical good-looking guy who knows it all. Muscles everywhere, cocky, a smile that could melt butter..." She paused. "I look back now and wonder what I saw in him. We dated—oh, I don't know. Maybe six months. He proposed with a big fancy diamond, and I said yes. I wanted to get out of my mother's house and have a real father for Damian. I figured it was time I had a life of my own." She looked straight at Summer. "People say yes for all kinds of reasons.

"I couldn't get pregnant for a while, though, almost four years, and that was the beginning. He wanted a child right away, and when that didn't work out...I started to see the real T.J. The one who drank and turned ugly when things didn't go his way." She crossed her arms.

"Even after Dinah was born, things didn't change too much. He always found something to get mad about. When Dinah was two, I finally got smart. I didn't want my daughter growing up in a house like that." She smoothed her hands over her lap. "So we moved away to start over."

"But now you're worried about him finding you?"

"He has a temper. T.J. isn't used to people telling him no, so when I asked for a divorce, he told me I'd be sorry. That he'd take Dinah from me if it was the last thing he did."

A car backfired somewhere close by, and Summer jumped. Now she was doubly glad she'd arranged the rental contingency with Sadie. At least the Knights could feel safe no matter what happened with the sale of the house.

"Enough about my problems." Hannah sipped her latte. The color came back into her face. "How did it go with those people who came to look at the house yesterday?"

Summer shook her head. "It needed too much work. They wanted something move-in ready."

Hannah shrugged. "Then they weren't the right people."

"I guess." *But I can't stay here and wait for the right people forever. I can't pick out curtains and play house like nothing else matters.* Guilt crowded Summer's heart. She'd asked her assistants back in San Francisco to shoulder so much of the responsibility. She'd put that part of her life on hold, thinking she needed all the answers here in Pine Point before she left again. But maybe she didn't. Maybe answers to long-gone nights, to relationships that had barely existed in the first place, were overrated.

Or maybe she was just afraid to face them head-on.

◌⃝

The red pickup truck gunned through the light, and Theo grabbed the door handle to keep from flying across the seat. "Jesus Christ. Keep it on the road, would ya?"

The guy behind the wheel grinned. "Shut the hell up. We only got thirty minutes for lunch, and I still gotta get a new drill bit if I'm gonna finish that job today." He careened onto Main

Street and slowed down, looking for a parking spot.

Theo cut a glance out the window. They'd ended up doing his boss's errand in Silver Valley—one of the towns he meant to scout out for signs of Damian. Looked like a pretty la-de-da place, with fancy stores and fancy sidewalk benches and restaurants that had tables outside, complete with umbrellas and tanned teenagers running plates of food back and forth.

The driver jerked the wheel and stomped on the brakes as a yellow sports car backed out of a parking spot in front of Paul's Hardware. He maneuvered the truck forward and back, but Theo could have told him from the start that it wasn't going in.

"Shit. Too small." He slammed the truck into reverse and craned his neck, waiting for a break in the traffic. "Can I go?"

Theo didn't answer.

"Hey! We ain't gonna make it back 'less we find a place to park." He swore under his breath. "Maybe I'll just double-park it and run in."

Theo barely heard the guy. He was staring at the coffee shop next to the hardware store. Outside, three tables clustered around planters overflowing with purple flowers. One table was empty. A young guy with a goatee sat at another, pecking on a laptop. And two women sat at the third, drinking coffee and talking like they were best friends. He rolled down the window to get a better look.

"Son of a bitch."

He'd found her. Without even trying, he'd found his ex-wife enjoying a cup of coffee right smack in the middle of downtown Silver Valley. He didn't know who the hell was with her, but it didn't matter. If she didn't live in town, she lived close by. He shouldn't have too much trouble tracking down where Hannah and Dinah lived and—as long as Damian wasn't around—convincing them to come back to Baltimore with him.

Theo wet his lips and smiled. He could hardly wait.

Chapter Thirteen

Summer examined the tile samples and closed one eye. Yesterday's shopping trip with Hannah had turned out better than she'd expected. They'd hit three more stores after lunch, returning to Pine Point late in the afternoon loaded down with bags and boxes. *So much for paying off my credit card bill.* It had been worth it, though. Today, rose-colored curtains waited to be hung in the front room, and she stood in the master bath before six different bathroom tiles, trying to decide which would look right. Mac had called in three extra guys to help him this week, so the exterior of the house was shaping up as well. Sadie had two buyers coming to look at it tomorrow afternoon, and Summer wanted as much as possible done before then.

"Mac?" Damian called from somewhere above her.

"Yeah." Heavy footsteps thundered down the central staircase.

Summer's chest tightened. She wanted to see him. She didn't want to see him. She didn't trust herself to keep her hands to herself if they ended up in a room together again. Nudging a turquoise tile into place, she closed one eye.

"Gotta pick up Dinah from soccer practice. Be back in a few."

"Okay."

A chill spiraled down her spine. God, she had it bad. Even

his voice turned her into a neurotic schoolgirl, peeking around corners.

"I think I like the turquoise," she said aloud. She piled the remaining tiles back into their box and lugged it into the center of the bedroom. Her stomach growled. She'd worked straight through lunch, handling two conference calls and trying to smooth out a mix-up with the Portland State Historical Society. Now four o'clock reminded her that a breakfast of day-old doughnuts and coffee left something to be desired.

The door slammed, and Damian stomped back inside.

"Thought you were leaving," Mac said from the front room.

"Car battery died. I think I left my lights on this morning."

"I'd offer you mine, but it's a mess. The back and the passenger seat are full of stuff."

Summer peeked into the foyer. Damian glanced at his dust-streaked watch. "Damn. She finishes in ten minutes. There's no way I'm gonna make it."

"What about your mom?"

"She went to Albany for the day to visit my great-aunt."

Summer cleared her throat. "I can pick Dinah up if you want. I'm done here, anyway."

"Really? You're sure?" Relief spilled across Damian's face. "I'd appreciate it. They play over at the elementary school, behind the baseball fields."

"I know where it is." She reached for her keys. "You don't think she'll mind?"

"Nah. Dinah's a little shy around strangers, but she likes you fine."

"Okay. See you in a bit, then."

"Thanks." At the foot of the porch stairs, she glanced behind her and waved. Damian stood with both thumbs hooked in his belt loops and the strangest expression on his face.

Practice had ended by the time Summer reached the soccer fields. An emerald carpet stretched out beneath the afternoon sunlight, empty except for one small figure and Joyce Hadley. Shoulders slumped, Dinah sat on a bench beside her coach and kicked at the grass.

Summer left the convertible running and walked over. "Hi, Dinah."

Joyce was jotting something on a clipboard. At Summer's voice, she looked up and shaded her eyes.

"Summer!" The girl darted from the bench and slid one small hand into Summer's.

"Sorry I'm late. Your brother had a problem with his car."

"It's okay." A warm shoulder pressed into Summer's leg.

Joyce set the clipboard aside. For a minute she said nothing. Then, tucking her hair behind her ears, she smiled— too brightly, Summer thought—and approached them. "I'm not really supposed to let her leave with anyone except her brother or her mother."

Summer slid an arm around Dinah. "I understand. But it's sort of an emergency—Damian's car wouldn't start, and he—"

"Yes, I heard you." Joyce nodded and frowned. "Still..."

Oh, come on, Summer wanted to say. *This is Pine Point. You know me, for God's sake. Everyone knows everyone.*

"I guess it's all right." Joyce kneeled and smiled up at Dinah. "Just this once, okay? But make sure and tell your brother that he should call me if he has to change his plans, all right?"

Dinah nodded.

"As a matter of fact, why don't you have him call me

anyway?"

Summer lifted one eyebrow. Joyce Hadley fishing for a guy? Some things in Pine Point really did stay exactly the same.

Dinah tugged on her hand. "Okay. Bye, Coach Joyce."

"Did you have fun today?" Summer helped Dinah fasten her seatbelt.

"I guess. Mallory Hawkins hogs the ball so I don't get to score very much. She and Taylor Boone think they're the best players on the team. They're not very nice sometimes."

"Hmm." Summer had known a few Mallorys and Taylors in her time. Back then, though, the snippy attitudes and cruel slights had taken place in the hallways and classrooms of Pine Point High rather than on the soccer fields. *Different year, different place, same story.*

She found a jazz station and adjusted the volume.

"I like this," Dinah said after a minute.

"The music, hon?"

Dinah traced the stitching on her seat. "Yes. And you picking me up from practice." Her dimples popped as she turned to face Summer. "I'm glad you moved here. I'm glad you own that house." The wind caught her hair and blew it into her eyes, and she laughed.

Summer said nothing as they eased to a stop back at the house. *I'm glad too.* The words flashed into her mind. But was she really? Or had everything become much more complicated since she'd stepped off the plane just days ago? Questions with no answers. Beginnings and middles and ends of relationships, all looped together and choking the sense out of her. She wasn't sure that coming back to Pine Point, even to collect her father's ashes and sell a rundown, mammoth house, had been a good idea at all.

"Summer?" A cool washcloth on her forehead. The sterile smell of antiseptic. An ache along the entire left side of her body. She moaned.

"Don't move." The voice soothed her, rocked her back toward deep slumber, and she welcomed it. But on the edge of sleep, right before she fell, she heard words she didn't understand.

"...can't give a statement to the police. She doesn't even know where she is... Yes, it's possible. Injuries look like she might have been. But until she regains consciousness, we won't know. The boy's confessed, hasn't he?"

Summer gave herself up to the waves of unconsciousness that pulled her in. It didn't matter, anyway.

Again. Always when she least expected it. Summer dropped her forehead to the steering wheel and squeezed her eyes shut. By now she was used to the flashbacks, though they still made no sense. She had to see Gabe again. She had to fit everything together inside her head before she went officially insane and they committed her to Silver Valley Hospital's mental ward.

Talk to him. That will clear things up. Make things easier. With a heavy heart, Summer climbed from the car. She could tell herself that all she wanted, but she had a sinking feeling that talking to Gabe wasn't going to make things easier.

Instead, she suspected it would only make things much more complicated.

Chapter Fourteen

Summer hung up with Gabe and tore a round loaf of rye bread into pieces.

"Coffee? Sure," he'd said. "How's tomorrow afternoon sound?"

So tomorrow it would be—her day of reckoning, of finding out once and for all what had happened to them that night so long ago. She took a long breath and tried not to think about how that would change things. How it would change everything.

She eyed the array of breads and vegetables spread across the counter, pulled a new serrated knife from its wrapping and began to slice off the top of another loaf. Damian, Mac and the extra hires had finished the kitchen—cabinets, appliances and all—the day before, and she was throwing a dinner party for Rachael and Cat to celebrate.

Hammering sounds came from somewhere above her, and she smiled and sliced a brick of sharp cheddar. Maybe the guys would want to stay for dinner. Her cheeks warmed. Maybe Damian would want to stay longer than dinner, even.

She placed the bread bowl and two plates of cheese in the fridge to chill, then unwrapped a container of fresh strawberries. She was about to set a pan on the stove to melt chocolate when her cell phone rang.

"Listen, Summer," Rachael chattered before she could say

hello, "I totally forgot I promised Mom and Dad we'd do the family thing tonight. Cat got roped into it too. Can we come over for dinner tomorrow? I'll bake a cake, bring some balloons, make it a real celebration."

"Oh. Um, okay." Summer stared at the food and tried to hide her disappointment. "Have fun. Tell your parents I said hi."

"I'm really sorry." Rachael feigned disappointment, but Summer knew what family dinners were like at the Hunter home. Stories shouted one over the other, food passed around the table, followed by card games and Monopoly and backgammon. Mr. Hunter took his backgammon very seriously; she'd lost her fair share of quarters to him back in middle school. What she wouldn't give to join in some of their raucous entertainment, even for a night.

"I'll talk to you tomorrow."

"'Kay." Summer slipped her cell phone into her pocket and reached across the counter, preoccupied. She wondered if the bread dip would keep. She wondered if she should open the big bottle of Merlot and celebrate anyway. Distracted, she closed her hand on the knife blade by mistake. "Ow! Dammit." Ruby drops seeped from between her fingers, and she reached for a paper towel and tried to stem the flow.

Too late. Memories came wheeling in before she could stop them.

"Summer?" Gabe lifted her chin. "Don't look down. Don't look anywhere but right here." He forced her to meet his gaze.

Her ankle hurt. Her face hurt, and every time she touched her forehead, her hand came away red.

She looked back at the car, but the windows were red too. And broken. She realized after a moment that the dark puddle at her feet wasn't water or engine oil. It was blood.

Summer fought for breath. *It's okay,* she tried to tell herself as the walls spun. *You are standing in a kitchen, not looking at your brother's broken body or a flashing red stoplight.* Didn't matter. The visions locked up her brain and she couldn't escape. Blood dripped from her palm, and her face flushed. A moment before she lost consciousness, she stumbled against the counter and tipped over the bowl of strawberries. Red drops fell to the floor all around her.

"Summer?" The voice came from far away. "Hey. Can you hear me?"

She struggled to sit up. Strong arms held her but she pushed them away. She blinked and tried to breathe. An instant later, Damian's face sharpened into view. Her tongue caught in her mouth, and she struggled to find words. "Wh-what happened?"

He brushed the hair from her eyes. "You tell me. I was working in the other room and heard you hit the ground."

She'd fainted? "How long was I out?"

"Couple minutes, maybe. Not long." He leaned close and she wondered if he meant to kiss her again.

She touched the back of her head. "Ouch." Suddenly, she noticed the strong smell that surrounded them. She pulled her hand away and examined the red color staining her fingers. Not blood. Thank God. "Just strawberries."

Damian glanced around. "Yeah, I guess you dumped them. No big deal. I can pick up more at the farm stand if you want."

To her surprise, Summer burst into tears.

"Hey." He pulled her to his chest and she let herself fall into the comfort of it. "It's okay." He murmured the words into her hair. "It's okay."

It wasn't okay. She wasn't sure it ever would be. The sobs came from deep inside her chest and made her throat hurt. "I'm sorry. I just—"

"Don't be." He laced his fingers through hers. "You've got a hell of a lot going on these days. You're entitled to a minor breakdown."

She nodded into his chest. He smelled good, like sawdust and soap. After a few minutes, her sobs subsided. She loosened her grip on his shirt and ran one hand through her hair. "God, I'm sorry." She wondered if she would ever feel normal in this place. She doubted it.

He glanced around and began to collect stray strawberries, tossing them one by one into the nearby garbage can. "Were you making something?"

"Trying to. Rachael and Cat are coming over for dinner." Then she remembered Rachael's call. "They were supposed to, anyway. She just canceled." She reached for a towel and scrubbed away the red spots that seemed to cover the new floor.

"Hey." Damian held out a hand and lifted her to her feet. "Leave it. I'll bring in some cleaner tomorrow."

"Oh. Okay." Summer abandoned the towel, now stained pink, and leaned against the counter. She still felt unsteady. Maybe this had been the wrong idea, moving into the house. Staying here at all. Every step seemed wrong.

Damian scratched his face and left a streak of dust from temple to jaw. When he grabbed the edge of his T-shirt to wipe his brow, Summer glimpsed rock-hard abs, slick with sweat. Just like that, her mind wheeled again, and doubt vanished, replaced by desire.

She took a deep breath. "Hey...would you like to stay for dinner, instead? I mean, I already have all this food and everything..."

"Ah, so I'm your second choice?" He propped an elbow against the new stainless steel refrigerator and grinned.

If you knew what my choice really was, I wouldn't be standing here talking about dinner, and you wouldn't have any clothes on. "Ah, no. Definitely not. I just figured you already had plans." She ignored the headache that was beginning to squeeze her temples.

"Nope. And I'd love to." He glanced down at himself. "I gotta run home and take a shower, though."

"Sure." She busied herself with wrapping a fresh paper towel around her hand. The image of Damian standing naked under a stream of water was threatening to shred away her last bit of self-control. "No rush."

"You sure you're all right? You hit the ground pretty hard. Don't want to have someone look at that bump on your head?"

Only you, she almost said. *You can look all you want. At whatever you want.* She bit her lip to keep from uttering the words out loud. Maybe she'd suffered some head trauma after all.

"No, it's fine. Thanks for rescuing, me, though."

"Anytime." He loped into the foyer and disappeared from view.

Anytime? Hope you mean that. Actually, she could probably use a shower of her own. A good cold one to shock the indiscreet thoughts from her mind once and for all.

က်စ်

"Hey there." A hour later Damian pulled open the back screen door.

"Hey yourself."

"How're you feeling?"

"Okay." Two Tylenol and a glass of wine had chased away her headache. The embarrassment of fainting in the kitchen might last a little longer, but he'd come back for dinner. That meant he didn't think she was a complete idiot, right?

Damian stopped on the threshold, inches away, and her gaze traveled downward before she could stop it. Faded jeans hugged muscular thighs. The brilliant white of a fresh polo shirt contrasted with his tanned arms. Faint scents of soap and deodorant mingled above the hint of sawdust and paint she'd come to associate with the house. With him.

"Looks great out here."

"Thanks." Summer had dragged the folding table from the kitchen onto the porch and tossed on a new checked cloth. No chairs, but she'd guessed they could sit on the steps. Better view of the yard and the setting sun, anyway. "Help yourself." Settling herself on the top step, she nibbled and sipped and waited to see where he would sit. How close.

"Heard my mom spent a lot of your money the other day." Damian sank onto the step beside her, his own plate piled high. Their legs brushed, and he didn't move away. Neither did she.

"Yeah, probably more than I wanted to, but that's okay. She was right about everything."

He cleaned the nachos from his plate. "She's good at that. Has a really keen eye."

"No kidding." Summer chased a stray strawberry around her plate. "You're lucky," she added. "My mom died when I was born."

Damian whistled. "Haven't had it easy, have you?"

"Stuff happens. I never knew it any other way."

"It's still a lousy break."

Summer studied her wineglass. A few feet away, she saw a braided rope of flowers Dinah had made for her earlier. The wildflowers twined around the railing, a little faded in the afternoon heat but still fragrant. "Your sister's adorable."

He popped two stuffed mushrooms into his mouth. "Yeah, she is." He paused. "Tries to set me up with all the wrong women, but she means well."

"Ah...like Joyce Hadley?" Summer recalled the look on Joyce's face when she'd picked up Dinah from practice.

He shrugged. "Dinah doesn't know too many women my age. She thinks we'd make a good couple, mostly because Joyce is blonde and has pretty fingernails. Oh, and makes a mean chocolate chip cookie."

Summer laughed. "That's not what does it for you?"

He glanced over. "What do you think?"

Her stomach tightened in desire, and a thrill of something unknown and desperately wanted spiraled down her spine. "Well, I do think Dinah has good taste," she joked. "All the Hadleys are beautiful. You might be missing your chance. Most of the guys in this town would give anything to go out with one of them."

"Yeah? Well, I'm not most of the guys in this town." His gaze steadied on her mouth. Shifting his weight on the step, he moved an inch or two closer and shaded his eyes against the sun. "So what was this place like years ago, anyway? When you and Mac were kids."

"The house? Or the town?"

"Both, I guess."

Summer didn't answer for a moment. *Ask me about San Francisco, and I'll give you a history lesson. I can tell you which restaurants have the best pasta or where to buy designer shoes at half the price. But Pine Point? It's too colored, too shaded, too jaded—or maybe I am—by everything that's happened in its shadows. What was this place like? I can't answer that without remembering what I was like. And I'm not sure I want to do that.*

She took a deep breath. "Well, this house was always a mess. Run-down for as long as I can remember. The story goes that a big steel family from New York City built it as a getaway sometime in the 1800s. Your house—the rental—was the caretaker's place. But when the only son died, the daughter who inherited it didn't want it, so I guess no one lived here after about 1920 or so. Weather and local kids took their toll on it after that. After a while, people just avoided it."

"The haunted house of Pine Point, huh?"

"It really was. In middle school, kids used to dare each other to come up on the porch and look in the windows. In high school, they'd sneak in and drink until the cops came by and threw them out." She remembered something else. "And sometimes couples came here. You could see the entire sky at night from one of the bedrooms upstairs."

"Can you see the Big Dipper?" Gabe ran his fingers along her bare collarbone.

Summer nodded, her palms damp with nerves and newfound love. The moonlight spilled through the cracked circular window and landed on the blanket they'd laid across the dusty floor. Two empty wine cooler bottles rolled at their feet. But it wasn't the sticky-sweet cherry alcohol that made her head spin. She was sure of that.

Gabe kissed her just below the ear, in the spot that always made her squirm, and then lower, along the curve of her shoulder. She stopped looking at the stars.

Summer's knee jittered with the memory, and she twisted her fingers together. Her gaze traveled upward to the window they'd lain beneath. *Wow.* She'd forgotten that night. How ironic. The very house she now owned she'd christened with teenage hormones years before. Maybe destiny had a stronger hand in things than she wanted to admit.

Damian rested his head against the porch railing and closed his eyes. The early evening sun played across the bridge of his nose, where a few freckles sketched a connect-the-dots from cheek to cheek. With his eyes shut and his mouth relaxed, he looked young, almost boyish. A sudden urge to reach over and kiss him seized her, and she sat on her hands to keep them where they belonged.

Behave yourself, Summer. At least for a little while longer.

He blinked and caught her looking. "Did you like going to school here? Knowing everything about everyone else?"

Summer propped her chin in one palm. "It was tolerable. Same as any other small town, I guess. Lots of stories and rumors, but most people had your back when you needed them to. What was it like growing up in Poisonwood?"

"Pretty damn boring."

They both laughed.

"You like working in construction?"

"It's a job." He shrugged. "I went to the junior college up north, got a degree in marketing. I'd like to use that someday."

"Yeah? Adirondack Community?"

He nodded. "I was doing odd jobs for a while when we first got into New York. I still like it, but I figured manual labor was gonna kill me if I did it for the next thirty years. So I went part-time while Mom was figuring out where she wanted to put down some roots." He smiled, but the expression didn't reach his eyes. "Took me almost three years to finish. And that was three years ago."

He reached over and brushed a strand of hair from her forehead. Summer's skin sizzled. He left his hand resting against her cheek, and she wanted to lean into it, to feel the impression of his palm deep down, where she'd felt cold and empty for so long.

"You're..." He didn't finish the thought. Instead he leaned over and lifted her chin. Hungry lips met hers, and she wasn't sure in the next instant whose hands moved first or whose voice rumbled low in the throat. All she knew was that she couldn't get close enough to him.

Their legs tangled. His fingers entwined with hers. One thumb stroked the tender skin of her palm before reaching down to caress a soft spot at the small of her back. She ran a hand over his hair, over the soft ridges in his ear and the bulk of his shoulder. He murmured something into her skin, a humming that set her nerves on fire. She let her head fall back, let him move from her ear to her neck to her collarbone in steps so slow and sweet she thought she might die from anticipation. Pinks and blues danced behind her eyelids.

She didn't want to open her eyes when he pulled back and let his hands rest on her waist. She wanted his mouth on hers again. Hell, she wanted his mouth in other places, and if it meant bare floor and sawdust and a sleeping bag, then so be it. But he didn't move. When she finally gave in and peeked, she saw him staring at her.

"Sorry." One dimple popped out. "That probably wasn't what you had in mind when you asked me to stay for dinner."

Summer traced the outline of Damian's bottom lip and the stubble along his jaw. Her hand fell to his lap, to the evidence that he'd felt agonizing pleasure from their kiss. In that moment it took all his self-control not to carry her inside, peel off every layer of clothing and make her come in the moonlight.

"Summer." He placed his hand on hers and, after a second, moved it to her own leg. "I didn't come here for that."

Her gaze dropped to the steps.

"Not that I don't want to."

"Then what is it?"

"I...ah, I just don't know if we should start something up if you're leaving soon."

"Oh. Right." She focused on the porch step between her flip-flops and reached out a fingernail to worry at a loose board. When her cell phone buzzed a moment later, she moved to the far side of the step and checked the message. The expression on her face changed.

"Everything okay?"

"Yeah. Just a text from Gabe."

"Roberts?"

She nodded.

Desire left him, just like that. "Your boyfriend back in school?"

"Well yeah, but now he's just—wait, you heard that?"

"Small town. Stories and rumors, remember?" Damian laced his fingers behind his head and asked the question he didn't want to know the answer to. "Something still there?"

She stared at him. "No. Not that it's any of your business."

"Hey, I was just asking."

"And I'm just answering." She stood and started carrying dishes inside.

He hurried to follow. "Summer, come on. I'm not a bad guy

for wanting to know."

"I guess." She ran water in the sink and arranged pans to soak.

"Just heard a few people talking and wondered what was true."

She turned around and leaned against the counter. Her guarded expression relaxed a little. "I don't know. I haven't heard what people are saying these days. But small towns stir up stuff that never existed. And they ignore what's right in front of them." Her shoulders lifted. "Yeah, there's history there. What else do you want me to say?"

Did he really kill your brother? Was he so drunk when the cops cuffed him he could barely stay on his feet? Damian had heard varying reports about Gabe Roberts and his role in the car accident from Mac and Cat and a few guys at the local watering holes. But he didn't dare put those questions into words. If half of it was true, he couldn't believe Summer would give that guy the time of day.

He shook his head and turned away. He wasn't sure he could risk getting involved with someone who had more ghosts than he did. "Maybe we should call it a night."

"Wait." She took his hand. "I'm sorry. I don't mean...it's just—it's so complicated, things with me and Gabe." She paused. "He was there the night my brother died."

"I know."

"And I...there are things I still need to sort out about it." She chewed her lower lip.

"That means seeing him."

"Yeah."

He cleared his throat. "Then maybe you should do that first and call me later."

"You're mad?"

"No. Just not willing to get in the middle of a messy past." He had one of his own. He wasn't sure he could take on anyone else's.

She stared over his shoulder and he thought tears rose in her eyes. "Okay. I get it."

Together they walked down the porch steps. Damian stopped at the bottom and stood below her, looking up. From here they met almost eye to eye. "Thanks for making dinner." He paused. "If you get things worked out or change your mind, let me know."

"Okay." Her voice remained flat, with little emotion.

The sun sank another inch below the trees. He wanted to say something else, but everything he worked up inside his head sounded stupid. "'Night, Summer," he finally said and headed for the path that led back to the farmhouse.

"Goodnight."

Chapter Fifteen

Summer woke early, before the sun had touched the hills. The sleeping bag was twisted around her waist, her pillow tossed to the side. Mourning doves cooed outside her window, plaintive and heart-rending. She sat up. Perspiration dotted her forehead and her upper lip. Her back ached. She heard no sound of Damian or Mac. *They aren't here yet. Good.*

She crossed her arms and closed her eyes again. She could still feel him. God, she could still *smell* him. Her desire hadn't diminished at all, even twelve hours later. A breath of air escaped her lips and she let the night play behind her eyelids. Jitters sang along her skin. If she lay there any longer, she'd remember every last whisper he'd passed across her lips.

But then he walked away from me. Her eyes flew open. He hadn't wanted to get involved. In fact, he'd as good as spun her in the direction of Gabe Roberts with his blessing. She bit her bottom lip. *Fine.*

The sun snuck its way over the horizon. Summer peeled off the sleeping bag and reached for her robe. She had to get out of here. She couldn't be in the house when the guys came by to start work. She supposed Damian had a point. Why get involved with the crazy woman who lived in the past and was leaving in less than a week?

She fished some running clothes from her suitcase and

skimmed her hair into a ponytail. She didn't want to be angry with him. But she didn't like saying goodbye in darkness. She didn't like waking up alone and wanting something she had no business asking for. And because she wasn't sure what she would say when she saw him, she thought she'd better just avoid him altogether.

She fastened her watch, double-knotted her laces and slipped out the back door. Mac had installed a new dead-bolt but she didn't bother to secure it. Everyone in Pine Point knew the house was in the middle of renovations, and if anyone snuck in, there wasn't much to steal anyway. She closed the door firmly and jogged through the backyard. She paused at the path that led to the farmhouse and then deliberately turned toward the sidewalk and shaded her eyes against the sun.

No sound. No cars. Only her own thoughts chattering inside her head. Summer headed away from the house and started to run.

ය80

Damian left the farmhouse early to pick up nails and screws at the hardware store over in Silver Valley. He didn't mind the drive, despite the fog that hung over the fields. He needed to clear his head, anyway. On the way back he stopped at the single gas station on the long stretch of road between the two towns. Inside, he managed to spill a stack of plastic cup lids, drop his change and slosh coffee onto the counter.

"You okay?" The cute brunette at the register pursed her lips and helped him pick coins off the floor.

"Yeah." But he wasn't. He hadn't slept much, just stared at the ceiling above his bed, where Summer looked down at him with inky eyes and asked him to stay to dinner, over and over again. *Did I make the right decision? Or just sound like an idiot with a twisted-up head?*

Back at the worksite he sat behind the wheel for almost ten minutes. His coffee had cooled to lukewarm by the time he joined Mac in the foyer.

"You're late."

"Sorry."

The heavyset man grunted. "'S okay."

A furtive glance at Summer's bedroom door revealed nothing. "She here?"

"Nope. Saw her jogging down by the school 'bout twenty minutes ago with Roberts. Looked like she had about a thousand things on her mind."

Jogging with Gabe Roberts? Damian strapped on his tool belt and tried to ignore the jealousy that stirred in his stomach. "Is all that shit really true?"

"All what shit?"

"About him killing Summer's brother."

Mac looked at him with an odd expression. "Happened a long time ago, man. No good comes from digging up stories."

"But it is, right?"

Mac shrugged. "He was DWI, word is, and didn't slow at the flashing yellow. Didn't even try to fight the sobriety test the cop gave him. But the other driver was drunk too, the guy who died later at the hospital. Tough to prove it was all Gabe's fault. And he had a good lawyer." He hefted a box onto his shoulder. "Sure, some people are still pissed about it. They think he should've at least moved someplace else, 'stead of coming back to Pine Point. They don't want to see him walking around alive and well while Donnie's lying in the ground."

Damian shook his head. "Jesus." No wonder Summer had

stayed away for so long. No wonder she carried around sadness half the time. He still didn't get why she'd be burning to spend time with her ex-boyfriend considering all that had happened, but he might as well give up guessing. Loss and forgiveness came in all kinds of packages.

He just wished he could get her out of his head instead of dwelling on the shape of her mouth or the taste of her skin or the way he wanted to be with her despite every rational thought that told him to run in the opposite direction.

CB80

Theo cradled his bleeding hand close to his chest and jerked the borrowed pickup into a space in front of the Adirondack Region Medical Clinic. This place was a little farther out than he'd originally thought, closer to Pine Point than Silver Valley, but apparently it was the closest thing to a walk-in urgent care center this area had.

"What a hick town." He spat out the open window and hoped it didn't take half the day to get his hand looked at. He suspected these backcountry places had a couple of nurses and one doc who drove in from Albany once or twice a week. The parking lot was almost empty, but a cop stood talking to some old lady in a Cadillac a few spots down. Theo took his time driving to a spot at the other end. He pulled in as the cop waved goodbye to Grandma and pointed his cruiser in the opposite direction. Good. The last thing he needed was some local boy nosing around his business.

He peeled the blood-soaked rag away from his left hand. "Damn." Less than a week on the job, and he'd managed to fall off a scaffolding and take a stray piece of metal through his hand. Wrenched his back something good too. He cursed his stupidity. If he didn't watch it, people would start paying more attention to him than he liked. With most injuries, he could pop a few aspirin, swig some bourbon and sleep it off. Not this one.

He elbowed open the door and limped through the clinic's lobby. A lady with her kid, a dirty brat with tear-stained cheeks, sat in two of the vinyl chairs. Balancing a clipboard on her knee, she filled out a form while the boy whined and rubbed his nose. One hand looked as if it had been badly burned.

Theo propped one elbow on the desk at the reception area. His back screamed with fresh pain. Perspiration trickled down his temples. Behind a glass window sat two women, one with white hair who looked like she was about to kick the bucket, and the other a good-looking girl in her early twenties. Neither looked up at him. After a minute, he rapped his knuckles on the glass. "Hey."

Grandma glanced up through glasses an inch thick, nodded and returned to her paperwork. The blonde spoke into the telephone receiver and held up one manicured finger in his direction. Behind him, the brat began to cry full-scale. Blood leaked through his makeshift bandage and dripped onto the counter.

"Hey!" This time he used his fist to pound. It worked. Blondie hung up the phone, saw the blood and jumped from her chair. Despite the pain clouding his head, Theo admired her firm, full breasts and the creamy skin that flushed as she handed him a towel. She grabbed a clipboard from the stack behind her.

"Nature of the injury?"

"Fell off a scaffolding," he said, gritting his teeth. "Landed on some metal, put a piece through my hand." *Just give me some Vicodin and I'll be fine.*

"Any other injuries?"

"Yeah, my back don't feel too great right about now."

She added that to her form.

"Insurance?"

"Don't have any. But don't worry, I've got cash to cover it," he added when he saw her pretty features frown.

"Well, we'll take care of that after the doctor sees you."

A nurse came into the waiting room and led away the lady with her screaming kid. Finally. Theo closed his eyes and let out a breath. Silence—much better. The pain in his back receded a fraction.

"Sir, are you okay? Would you like some water?"

Theo nodded. "That'd be good."

She led him to a chair, then patted him on the shoulder and took her clipboard and her fine ass back behind the desk. A minute later, she reappeared with a paper cup of water. Theo drained it in one gulp.

"It'll just be a few minutes," she promised.

"Miss?"

She turned.

"What's your name?"

She smiled. "Joyce. Let me know if you need anything else."

Theo nodded and closed his eyes. Might as well catch a nap. A waiting room was as good a place as any.

"How'd you make out?" Joyce asked as he left the curtained treatment area two hours later.

Theo held up his bandaged left hand in response.

"How's your back?"

"They x-rayed it. Nothin' broken."

"Well, that's good." She tapped the keyboard and studied the computer screen in front of her.

"Say, can I ask you somethin'?" Theo leaned closer and dropped his voice, though the old lady behind the desk had disappeared and no one else sat in the waiting room.

"Sure."

"Any chance you know someone named Hannah Knight?"

Joyce stopped typing and wrinkled her pretty features in concentration. "Well, I live over in Pine Point. But I don't think I've heard that name before."

"Got a phone book?"

She fussed under the counter and came up with a slim yellow book. "Here you are."

It took him less than a minute to see that the only Knight number listed in Silver Valley belonged to a Mamie and Herb.

"I do know a *Damian* Knight," Joyce offered as she took back the phone book. She pinked with the confession, and Theo wondered if Damian had spent a night or two in the blonde's bed. Wouldn't be surprised.

"Oh, yeah?" He kept his voice as calm as he could. "He live in Pine Point or Silver Valley?"

She glanced down, and he knew he'd pushed too far. "I don't really, well..." She clammed up.

He'd come on too eager, he knew in an instant. She typed something and stared at the computer screen, and he knew he wouldn't get anymore out of her. Didn't matter. She'd as good as spilled the fact that Damian lived in Pine Point, and Theo would put money on the fact that Hannah and Dinah weren't far away. "Hey, you know, don't worry about it. I got Hannah's cell number somewhere."

Joyce printed something out and slid the paper across the desk to him. Her smile seemed a little less warm than before. "That's the total. You can pay it all now, or we can set up a monthly billing system if you'd prefer."

He straightened, though his back still felt like it was about to cramp up. "Nah, I told you I got the cash." He dug into his back pocket, pulled out his wallet and separated some wrinkled hundred-dollar bills. "Here."

She counted them carefully and handed him a few singles in change. "There you are."

"Thanks."

"Mm hmm." Eyes cast down, Joyce returned to her filing without another word.

Theo laid rubber leaving the parking lot. The effects of the pain medication started to kick in and he grinned. A few more hours on the job this afternoon, and then he could lose himself in a bottle of Jack Daniels. Might take a drive over to Pine Point later on and see what that shitty little town looked like. And maybe tomorrow or the day after he'd stop in the local diner, ask around and find out where exactly Hannah was calling home. Or where Damian was working. At this point he'd take either one. Fact was, he almost welcomed the chance to stand face-to-face with Damian and remind him which one of them was in charge.

Theo gunned the truck through a red light and flipped off a woman in a minivan who beeped her horn at him. *Patience,* he told himself. *That's all I need.*

Chapter Sixteen

"I think your sister's right about Summer." Hannah Knight dropped a second pork chop onto Damian's plate. From the living room came the sound of Dinah's favorite evening television show and the little girl's laughter.

Damian felt his cheeks redden. He ran a slice of garlic bread around his plate and sopped up gravy. "I don't know what you're talking about."

"Please. Dinah adores her. Loves spending time at the house. She's thrilled that Summer picked her up from practice." She cocked her head. "And it seems to me you keep some awfully long hours on that job."

Damian reached for the peach cobbler his mom had made for dessert. "Don't have much choice. Mac wants to have it finished by Labor Day. Even with the guys that helped out last week, we're behind."

When Hannah remained silent, he glanced up. A smile played on her face, and bright blue eyes sparkled at him.

"What?" He didn't like that look, the one that speared through his skin and into the deepest part of his heart. Try as he might, he couldn't keep anything from his mom. She caught every emotion that rumbled through his life. She knew when he hurt, when he needed space, when sleep evaded him or when he felt like jumping for joy. He busied himself with forking up pieces of cobbler and willed his mind blank.

Hannah slipped into the chair opposite him and rested her elbows on the table. "Summer seems a little lonely, if you ask me."

"She just lost her father. And she's back in the place where her brother died. With a house she doesn't want." *And an ex-boyfriend who's still in the picture.* He frowned and drank an entire glass of iced tea without stopping.

Hannah smiled. "That's all the more reason for you to take her out, spend some time with her while she's here and keep her mind off things."

"Ah, I...I'm not really interested," Damian lied. He couldn't afford to be.

"Why not? She's attractive. Intelligent. Successful too." She laid a hand on his wrist. "You can't shut yourself off forever."

"I'm not." Couldn't his mother just accept that he didn't want to get involved? "She's got something going on with Gabe Roberts, anyway."

Her forehead dipped in concentration. "Who's that? Someone here in town?"

"Yeah."

"Oh." She didn't say anything after that.

Damian pushed his chair back and slammed his knee against the table. His mom meant well, but she didn't understand. Gabe wasn't the only reason Damian was keeping his distance, though he wasn't about to step on the toes of the guy who knew her better than anyone else in Pine Point. Summer was leaving in less than a week. She had a whole other life on the other side of the country. The bottom line was, he didn't trust himself to take her out once or twice and then say goodbye. A few kisses had sent his mind reeling. He could only imagine what an entire evening with her would do.

A sleepy Dinah smiled at Damian as he poked his head into the living room an hour later.

"Hey, ladybug."

"Hey." She'd tucked a blanket around her legs and curled into the corner of the sofa.

"Ready for bed?"

She nodded, eyelids heavy.

Damian smiled and took her hand as they climbed the stairs. Though she seemed to grow an inch every day, this was still their bedtime ritual, the one he'd started when she was only a few months old. Back in Poisonwood, she'd stopped sleeping for a while as an infant. Between a rough bout of colic and his mom and T.J. fighting, she wailed all night in her crib. Only Damian's voice singing lullabies in the darkness could soothe her. Seven years later, he hoped it still did.

Damian tucked Dinah into her twin bed and pulled the pink-and-white curtains closed.

"Dame?"

"What?"

"Can I come to work with you tomorrow?"

He switched on the pink nightlight to keep the bogeyman away. "We'll see."

"I like it when Summer's there." The girl propped herself up on one elbow. "I hope she stays for a while. Do you think she will?"

"I don't know, sweetie." Damian hid a smile. First his mother, now his sister. Seemed like all the women in his life wanted to match him up with the one person he absolutely, positively could not get involved with.

Dinah lay back down and pulled the sheet up to her chin.

Damian lifted his guitar from its case in the corner and ran his fingers lightly over the strings. He took a minute to tune it, then settled himself in the chair by the door and began to play. He never needed the light or any music to read. He just listened to his heart and let its rhythm move his fingers. Sometimes he played Dinah's old favorites, children's songs she knew every word to. Other times he relied on the Beatles or Elton John, depending on his mood.

Tonight, he played his own composition, a new tune that had been running around his brain the last few days. The notes rippled through the room like slow-moving water, and Damian hummed as the line took shape beneath his fingers.

In a few minutes, Dinah's breathing deepened, but Damian played on. The bridge formed itself. The chorus turned into something in a minor key. Pieces of lyrics sharpened inside his head. Closing his eyes, he let the notes fall, painting a landscape of brilliant color in his mind's eye. He hadn't written anything in a long time, but tonight the song almost composed itself.

When the last note hung in the air, he sat in the dark and let his heart return to normal.

○§◎

Past midnight, the telephone rang.

Damian jerked awake, clutching at the sheet. He sat up and looked at the clock. One-fifteen. It rang again and he lunged for the cordless extension in his room before Dinah or his mother awoke. Fear squeezed an icy fist around his organs. Telephone calls after midnight rarely meant anything good.

"Hello?"

Silence answered him.

"Hello!" His fingers, slippery with adrenaline, clung to the receiver.

Still Damian heard nothing. Then something mechanical clicked, and a low panting into the phone ran chills up his spine. He glanced at the Caller ID screen, but it read *Private Number*.

You son of a bitch.

"T.J.? That you?"

"Sure as shit is. Been a while."

Damian hadn't heard the voice in years, but it sounded exactly the same: slurred and pissed off.

He found us. Jesus Christ, he found us. Damian crept to the window and peered outside. No moon. No stars. T.J. could have been sitting fifty feet from the house, and Damian wouldn't have known it. He'd never believed in guns before, but in that moment he wished for a trigger in his hand. He'd point it straight at the guy's head without thinking twice.

"You know she's got a restraining order against you," he lied. "You come anywhere near us, the police'll dump your ass in jail."

"Oh, yeah?"

"Yeah. You need a personal invitation to your own funeral?" *Come and get it, asshole. I'll take care of you before the police ever have a chance.* "I'll kill you myself if I have to."

"You and whose army?"

"Did you hear me?" Worse than feeling T.J.'s fists on his back, worse than watching him shove Hannah across the room, was the thought of his threatening presence somewhere out there, close by. "I'm calling the police."

At that, the line went dead. Across the hall, Dinah

167

mumbled something in her sleep. The floorboards creaked beneath him, and Damian knew the call had woken his mother too. He threw the phone across the room, where it hit the wall and fell onto the carpet with a soft thud. He punched his pillow, imagining T.J.'s face in the wrinkles of cloth beneath his fist. Sleep had fled, probably for good, and in its place rage grew in his belly. A simmering fire spread to his chest and up through his lungs until he thought he would either scream or vomit in anger.

He retrieved the phone and dialed 911, knowing it probably wouldn't do any good. Wherever he'd called from, T.J. wasn't stupid enough to get caught near their house.

If he knew where their house was.

Damian folded himself in half. They'd done everything they could—relocated, changed their phone number, started a new life under the protection of a custody agreement that prevented T.J. from ever seeing Dinah again. He didn't care about them. He couldn't. All that man cared about was getting drunk and living off the government's money. He couldn't possibly want to be a father to Dinah. Why couldn't he accept the shambles he'd made of his life and move on?

Chapter Seventeen

"Hey." Gabe pulled out the chair opposite Summer and smiled.

She smiled in return; she couldn't help it. He still had it, that way of harnessing the sun and turning her whole day bright. "Hey yourself." She pushed a cup of coffee across the table as he sat and cracked his knuckles. "Ordered yours."

"Thanks." He dumped in two packets of sugar. "How's the house?"

"Better every day."

"Got any buyers yet?"

"Couple of people looking. It's huge, you know. Big price tag for Pine Point."

He nodded. "I remember people talking when your father bought it."

She wrapped both hands around her mug. "Yeah? Talking like he was crazy?"

"Nah. Just wondering." He took a sip. "I think it was his way of making amends. With himself, with the town. With you too, I guess, though he never got around to telling you that."

"That's what Joe tried to say."

"You don't believe him?"

She shrugged. "I don't know what to believe. My father was

so angry after the accident. The couple of times I talked to him, we fought." She glanced around the coffee shop, glad for its emptiness. "After a while I stopped calling."

"Then he leaves you a house."

"Exactly. And unless someone around here can communicate with ghosts, I don't think I'm ever gonna know why."

"Maybe you should stop asking why." Gabe tilted his head, and Summer found herself watching the dimples that had stolen her teenage heart. "Maybe if there aren't any answers, you just have to move on."

"When did you get so philosophical?"

He grinned. "Spent a lot of time thinking after you left."

"And?"

"And decided that we gotta deal with what life gives us. No use looking backwards." He paused. "Course I guess it's probably harder for you, since that's what you do for a living."

"Look backwards?" No one had ever phrased it that way. Summer frowned. Maybe Gabe was right. Maybe she needed to turn and start facing forward. But she couldn't do that until—

The door behind them opened and a teenage couple walked into the coffee shop. They held hands, fingers wrapped tightly as they glanced at the order board and chose matching skim lattes while barely looking away from one another.

"Think we were ever like that?" Summer's voice broke into his thoughts.

He smiled. "Nah. I was much better looking."

She stuck out her tongue. "Me too."

"You still are." Gabe didn't know how he felt about her, or about them, only that sitting across from Summer Thompson over a cup of coffee gave him a feeling of peace he hadn't had in a long time. Maybe ever.

She looked at the table and shook her head. "I'm a mess."

"You look pretty put together to me."

"I used to think so." She spoke to her mug. "Then I came back here. Now I keep having these flashbacks that put me right into that night all over again. I can hear Donnie. I can see you—and me—and the car. And the cops. But then—God, there are these awful holes too." She lifted her chin and grief filled her eyes. "*I can't remember what happened.* I have no goddamned memory of it at all. Was it my fault? Did I distract you? Did I do something to... I keep feeling like I did."

Gabe chose his words carefully. He'd come here meaning to tell her the truth. He'd convinced himself that full disclosure was his only choice. If she didn't hear it from him, she'd hear more stories from someone else. But the longer he sat there with her hand in his, the more he lost his nerve. He couldn't bear to break her heart a second time.

"It wasn't you. Mr. Hartwell was drunk. He ran the flashing red light." He shrugged. "And anyway, he died the next day in the hospital."

Summer sucked in a breath. "Wait—what?"

"Max Hartwell didn't make it. Had a massive heart attack after he got to the hospital. You knew that, right?" He wasn't sure what difference it made, all these years later. Neither of them had been close to the man.

"But my father—and Rachael said—" She raised a hand to her mouth. Her eyes widened. "Oh my God."

Confused, Gabe tried to read her face. He couldn't. "What?"

"Rachael said once, 'At least someone went to jail for it.' No matter what I could or couldn't remember, at least someone paid for killing Donnie. I thought she meant the other driver. Mr. Hartwell." She murmured the words, and tears filled her eyes. "But she meant you. Right? Because if he died—"

Gabe's chest constricted. "Yeah." He thought somehow she knew that he'd served time. "Two years for involuntary manslaughter. Not that long."

"You never told me." Her eyes widened. "Why? Why didn't anyone tell me that you went to jail?"

"You'd gone through enough. You needed to heal."

She shook her head slowly, back and forth. "But you did that...two years...and I never knew."

Gabe rubbed the back of his neck. Now he could never tell her the rest. She looked as though she'd seen a ghost. She didn't need any more of the details of that night. He could carry them around inside his skin forever. It got easier every day, anyway.

Summer's hair fell around her face, and her mouth trembled. "Oh, Gabe, I'm so sorry."

That, he found, was enough.

Cঞৎচ

"Tell me again why you're rushing back to the west coast." Joe Bernstein spread butter across a piece of bread.

Summer spun her straw and looked around the diner. She could barely meet the man's gaze. Why hadn't he told her about Gabe? Why hadn't *someone*? Why had everyone assumed she was too weak to know? "Well first, I'm not exactly rushing. I've been here for almost two weeks. And second, that's where my job is. I never meant to stay this long. It was only going to be a few days."

The lanky lawyer rested his elbows on the table. "Funny how that works out, isn't it? How the past pulls you back before you realize it."

I'm not sure funny is the word for it. Frustrating, maybe. Strange. Not really funny, though. "I'm not meant to be here, Joe. Besides, that house is too big for one person to live in. The major work's almost done. Sadie has everything in line—I don't have to be here to sell it. And it needs someone with a family who can fill it up with all the things I can't. That was my plan all along."

"You know, family isn't always made up of parents. Or brothers and sisters and aunts and uncles."

"You know what I mean."

The waitress brought their entrees and Joe leaned back in his chair. Steam rose in twisted wafts, obscuring his face in the dim light of the Corner Lounge restaurant. Summer tried but she couldn't read his eyes.

"I told you I was retiring from teaching at the college, right?"

She nodded.

"Which means they'll be looking for someone to take over those two classes in the fall." With deliberate strokes, Joe sliced his steak sandwich.

"Well, I'm sure they'll find someone, though your shoes are going to be tough to fill." Summer's stomach growled, and she savored the ravioli before her as if it were her last meal.

"I recommended you."

Her fork dropped to the plate. "What?" She stared at Joe and waited for the rest of the joke. "Oh, no. I can't," she went on when he said nothing. "I told you—I'm leaving."

He held up a hand. "Let me finish. The Adirondack

Historical Society has talked for some time about establishing a small museum in this area. Last week, they got the grant funding they've been working on for almost four years." He winked. "Who better than you to help get them up and running? You know everything about Pine Point, Silver Valley, the entire county area. You might even consider using the house as part of the museum itself. Do some research, use some of the grant money to restore the rooms with reproductions of period furniture. People love touring old homes. You know that. Then you can teach on the side."

"I can't."

"Why not?"

Frustration tied her stomach into knots, and her appetite fled as quickly as it had come. "Okay, I guess I came back for more than just to look at the house. I thought I could say hello to some old friends. Maybe even see my brother's grave. Then fly home again, no problem." She drew in a long breath. "But I just feel like being in Pine Point has pulled me under again. I thought I could face all the old memories and move on. But I can't. And I can't stay here every day waiting for it to get better. Because what if it doesn't?"

The worst part was, the old memories had failed her. They hadn't been the truth at all. Rearranging her understanding of what had happened all those years ago overwhelmed her. Staying in Pine Point permanently would only make her feel as though she were suffocating, every single day.

Joe studied her. "You know, the past only shapes us as far as we allow it to..."

She shook her head.

"...but it's the stuff of history books and museum exhibits." He placed one hand on hers. "It shouldn't be the way we frame our lives. You know that more than anyone. Learn from it, and then let it go. The present and the future...well, that's up to us."

෨

"You're confirmed for Tuesday at three," said the woman on the other end of the line. "One stop in Chicago, landing in San Francisco at seven fifty local time."

Summer nodded, relieved. Four more days and she'd be finished in Pine Point. She'd be heading west, where she belonged. She sent a quick text message to her assistant at the museum and another to Rachael. Maybe they could meet up for lunch one more time before she left.

She watched Joe pull away from the diner and raised her hand in goodbye. Stay in Pine Point? Help open a museum and take over teaching at the college? *No way.* She checked her watch as she turned toward the center of town, glad she'd left her car a few blocks away. *The walk will do me good.* She kept her gaze straight ahead while a thousand thoughts slipped in and out of her mind. Gabe. The accident. Her brother. Damian. She clenched a fist against her side. *No. Not Damian.* Nothing to think about there. She couldn't afford the luxury.

She'd almost reached the public parking lot when a strange man stopped her. "Excuse me." Clad in work clothes and heavy boots, he leaned against the front of Flo's Fold 'n' Fluff with the stub of a cigarette in his fingers.

"Ah, yes?"

The man stomped out his butt with a dirty toe and nodded a curt hello. She didn't know him, had never seen him around town. Of course, a lot of people had moved here in the last ten years, so that didn't mean much. From the way he was dressed, she guessed he was probably working on one of the many housing developments going up around Pine Point and Silver

Valley. Or maybe one of the never-ending road construction projects. *Seems like all I do is dodge orange cones these days.*

Despite his garb, though, the man appeared handsome, with a muscular build and steel-colored eyes that crinkled at the corners. He crossed his arms, cocked his head and ran his tongue over his bottom lip. "Can I ask you a favor? I'm lookin' for an address. Old buddy of mine."

"Um...sure." *I haven't lived here in a really long time,* she was about to say, *so I'm not sure I can help you,* but then he went on.

You know the way to County Route 78?"

"Sure. That's about the one place I do know."

"Just in town for a couple-a days, trying to look up a friend." He held out a hand. "Name's Theo."

Summer took it and squeezed for a quick moment. "Hi. Who's your friend?" Maybe it was one of the neighbors down the road from her place. She hadn't met all of them, though she'd been meaning to stop in and say hello.

"You gotta name?" he asked without answering. He ran his other hand over gelled hair.

"Um...Summer." Suddenly uncomfortable, she backed up a step.

Nodding, he let his gaze drop to her waist and back up again.

"Here, let me write down the directions for you," she said, digging into her purse for a pen and trying to finish the conversation.

"Don't bother. I remember everything." Theo stuffed his hands into his pockets and waited.

"Oh." Her hand dropped. "Okay. Turn right at the end of this block, onto Main Street. Follow Main out of town. Turn right onto Hanford, then a quick left onto 78. It's about a mile or so past the ball fields."

Theo's lips moved, and he repeated her directions under his breath. "Got it." In the moment before he disappeared, his eyes seemed to change, to turn gray and cold. "Thanks for the directions."

An hour later Summer slipped into the master bathroom of her house and peeled off her sticky shorts and tank top. She hadn't seen Damian in a couple of days, which was probably just as well. She didn't know what to tell him about Gabe, and she was still planning on leaving next week...so where did that leave things?

Nowhere, echoed the voice inside her head. *Nowhere at all.*

She stepped into the adjoining bathroom, also completely finished now, and ran a washcloth over her face and under her arms. She still felt as though she might break whenever he looked her way. She still felt all shaken up and fizzed over when she replayed their kisses in her head, as though no one had ever kissed her before. And she had no idea what to do about that.

She pulled on a pale blue sundress and brushed her hair. In bare feet, she made her way out onto the front porch. Beautifully refinished, its cherry steps and railing gleamed in the late afternoon sun. She smiled and looked around. She'd promised to meet Dinah for a tea party at four o'clock sharp. At least her friendship with the young girl hadn't slipped away as well.

"Summer?" The voice, high-pitched and eager, called her name. Thirty seconds later, Dinah appeared from around the corner of the house.

Summer waved at the girl with the muddy knees and the

177

wide grin. Dinah waved in return, though one hand remained behind her thin back. She skipped across the lawn and took the long way around the tall oak tree. Under its branches, she got tangled up and had to stop for a moment. Summer laughed. Finally Dinah slowed and climbed the porch steps, out of breath. At the top, she pulled her hand from behind her back.

"Here." Dinah presented her with a fistful of wildflowers. The stems were still damp. Purples and yellows and pinks poked out in all directions.

Summer took the bouquet and felt a tightness in her chest. "These are for me?"

Dinah nodded.

"Thank you, sweetie. They're beautiful." An odd lump rose into the center of her throat.

Dinah beamed. Her gangly legs stuck out from her denim shorts, and her bony elbows were scuffed with grass stains. *Only their eyes are different.* Unlike Damian's dark blue ones, which matched the color of Pine Point Lake at dusk, Dinah's were a deep brown, almost ebony, and her lashes endless.

She crouched to a seat beside Summer. "The porch looks really good."

Summer laid the flowers on her lap and ran one hand along the smooth wooden step. "Yes, it does. Your brother did a good job."

Damian and Mac had finished the front porch over the weekend. Dinah was right: it looked good. Actually, Summer thought, it looked more than good. It looked magnificent. The wide steps, the intricate carvings at the tops of the columns, the long lines of the porch as it stretched from end to end of the house—it all almost took her breath away. She'd gotten so used to entering and exiting through the back door that she'd almost forgotten about the front. This entrance seemed too fine to use everyday. She glanced behind her. Yesterday the double front doors that her father had special-ordered from Chicago had arrived, and Damian had stayed late to hang them. The entire façade of the house was complete.

Dinah leaned against Summer's knee, and Summer found herself rubbing the girl's back. Her fingers felt every bump in Dinah's spine. *Skin and bones. I used to be exactly the same way.* Skinny as the day was long, she hadn't blossomed until tenth grade, when all the other girls—the Hadleys, anyway, and their friends, the girls who really mattered—had been wearing size 34B bras for years, along with miniskirts that showed off womanly hips and thighs. Summer, on the other hand, had stared into the mirror every day from the moment she turned thirteen, wishing on the stars for curves in the right places. She hoped fate would be a little kinder to Dinah. Sometimes nature wasn't very nice.

Summer bent down and whispered into the girl's ear. "I have a surprise for you."

Dinah's head swiveled around. "What is it?"

"It's upstairs. It's a secret." And really, it was. Summer had discovered it just that afternoon, in her wanderings through the east wing of the third floor. The guys hadn't tackled that floor yet, because it needed the least amount of work.

Dinah followed her upstairs, one small damp hand in her larger one. The sun slanted across the floor and Summer wondered again about the people who'd lived here all those years ago. Along this hallway, a smooth groove had been worn in the wood. A chip nicked the otherwise clean lines of the wall. A crack worked its way down the length of the banister. *Marks from another lifetime, kind of like the ones that scar your heart across the decades.*

"Here." At the back of the far bedroom, Summer slid her

179

fingers along the wall until they found a seam. She reached up with one hand, down with the other, and pushed.

A door slipped open.

Dinah's jaw dropped. "What's that?"

A cracked round window at the back of the space cast a thin line of sun into the shadows. Summer had tested the floorboards earlier. Though dusty and warped, they held solid. "It's a secret room."

In her youth she'd heard stories about the house harboring fugitives on the Underground Railroad. Though pretty far north, the town of Pine Point would have made a good final stop for slaves fleeing to Canada. She looked around the room. If it were true, she'd just uncovered a gold mine in the eyes of potential buyers. Most homes that could prove a connection to that historic period were listed on national registries, protected and valued far above regular market price. She'd have to do a little more digging downtown and see what she could find out.

"Neat, isn't it?"

The ceiling slanted low as it met the eaves. From the outside, Summer suspected, it would look as though this back bedroom simply extended the full space; since the hideaway was merely ten square feet, the naked eye would never be able to tell the difference. A familiar thrill coursed through her. She loved discoveries. She loved history that took shape in actual things, wood and stone you could put your hands on. She'd spent her life researching places like this. To own a slice of the nineteenth century, even for a few weeks, was the closest she could ever hope to be to nirvana.

Dinah wandered from one end of the small room to the other. She ran her fingers over some ancient marks carved into the wood. "Did people live in here?"

Summer cocked her head. Eight might be a little young to

be hearing about the cruel side of the slave trade, she decided. "More like kids played in here. Hid from their parents. Made up stories and games on rainy days."

Dinah grinned. "Like me."

"Just like you." Summer rubbed the dust from the streaked glass window. From here she could make out only a square of grass and an arc of sky. Something like a chill passed along her arms. Yes, history had taken its toll here. She could feel it.

"I like it," Dinah said from behind her.

"Me too."

"Can it be just our secret?"

"Absolutely." She dropped a kiss onto Dinah's messy hair. "And now I think it's about time for our tea party." They slipped back into the bedroom, and Summer's lungs expanded with fresh air. A little too claustrophobic for her taste. She wondered if she'd made a mistake, showing it to the little girl.

But Dinah giggled to herself as they descended the stairs, and the secret room seemed long forgotten by the time they reached the first floor. Her smile changed. "I invited someone else to our tea party."

"You did?" Summer put a hand on Dinah's shoulder as they stepped over boxes. "Who?"

But when they stepped onto the porch, she had her answer. Twenty yards away, Damian was grilling burgers on a portable grill, stainless steel and shiny in the sun. She'd never seen it before. He looked over at her and winked. Butterflies swooped inside her stomach. He lifted the grill cover, and trails of smoke escaped, floating up to the sky.

"They're done," he said.

"I'll get the salad," Dinah piped up.

Salad? Summer looked from the girl to her brother and

back again.

"Dinah, go wash your hands at the hose out back first." Damian approached the porch.

"She doesn't have to use the hose." Summer laughed. "Come inside and use my bathroom."

"Okay." Dinah slipped inside.

"You didn't have to do that." Damian climbed the first two steps and stopped.

"She's a *girl*," Summer said with mock condescension. "She shouldn't have to use the hose the way you guys do." She crossed her arms. "Savages."

Damian laughed out loud and his dimples winked in the sun. She loved the way it sounded, carefree and full, from way down deep in his belly.

"Yup, that's me. Guess I'll go clean up out back, then," he said, "with the other savages."

Summer dropped her arms. "I was kidding."

Dinah stood in the doorway, cheeks pink. "Summer?"

"What's up, ladybug?" Adopting the nickname she'd heard Damian use, she slung an arm around the girl's shoulders. Dinah wrapped her own arm around Summer's waist, and together they walked into the kitchen.

"Do you like my brother?" she asked.

Summer pulled open the refrigerator door. Inside sat a wooden salad bowl, overflowing with greens. *When did they plan this?* She saw a plate of homemade chocolate chip cookies and wondered if Hannah was in on the secret tea party-slash-BBQ dinner as well. She bumped the door closed with her hip. "Of course I like your brother, sweetheart. Why?" She steadied her voice.

Dinah leaned against a counter and studied Summer with

thoughtful eyes. "I think you should be his girlfriend."

Summer kept her face averted as she rummaged in a drawer for some utensils. "Oh, I can't be Damian's girlfriend."

"Why not?"

How did she answer that? *Because the way he makes me feel scares the hell out of me. Because he thinks I still have feelings for another man.* "Because I'm only in town for a little while."

Dinah pouted.

"But your brother and I are good friends," Summer lied, "and that's better than being a girlfriend, because friends can be friends for a very long time." An eight-year-old couldn't read her face the way her twenty-six-year-old brother could, Summer hoped. She found some paper plates and napkins and hefted the salad bowl under one arm. Through the back windows she could see Damian rinsing off his arms and face. He'd removed his T-shirt, and a broad, bare chest glistened with heat and wetness. Water flew everywhere as the hose snaked through his hands. She almost dropped the salad tongs.

"But do you think you would be Damian's girlfriend if you lived in Pine Point for real?" Dinah followed Summer back through the house and out onto the porch again.

"You have a lot of questions today."

"Dame says it's good to ask questions," Dinah retorted as she laid the cookies on a paper plate. "It means you're smart."

"Well, your brother is right," Summer said, "but—"

"Right about what?" Damian scooped up the burgers onto paper plates, handed them to Summer and Dinah and joined them on the porch.

"Nothing. Your sister and I were having a girls' talk, that's all."

Dinah beamed and inched as close to Summer as she could without actually climbing into her lap. For a while, the three sat without speaking as the last rays of sun glowed down on them. Summer glanced at brother and sister. Even the way Damian and Dinah crossed their legs and balanced their plates on one knee, the left one, matched. A sudden sadness seized her.

"That's Mom," Damian said when a horn beeped. He glanced down at his watch. "Time for you to go, ladybug."

Summer's breath caught, and she almost wanted the girl to stay, just to run interference. She bit her lip instead and patted Dinah on the back.

Dinah helped herself to two cookies. "Okay." She reached over and hugged Summer. "Bye."

Summer's heart warmed at the unexpected embrace. "Bye, sweetheart." She spied a small yellow car idling beyond the shrubbery. "Tell your mom I said hi, okay? I'll see you soon."

Dinah skipped down the last four steps. An unruly ponytail bobbed at the back of her neck as she ran across the lawn. "Hi, Mom." Her faint, cricket voice floated on the air and was lost in the rumbling of the engine. A door creaked open and then slammed shut. The car pulled away from the curb, and they were gone.

Summer sat on the top step and stared up into the sky. Damian had disappeared inside, but she didn't really mind. She needed a few minutes to collect herself and calm her racing pulse. She could still smell his cologne in the air beside her and feel the warmth of his body only inches away. If he hadn't gotten up, she would have peeled off her clothes just to feel his skin on hers.

She inhaled, taking in a good long breath of clear Pine Point air. This she would miss. The air and the view of the stars at night. A San Francisco skyline could never take the place of bright white dots skating to eternity in the black above you. She raised one finger and moved it through the growing darkness, tracing the constellations she knew so well. Wrapping her arms around her knees, she peered again toward the street. Nothing but faint streetlights winked back.

The front door opened and closed. "You're quiet."

"Just thinking about how good this place looks," she lied. "About how much you and Mac have done this summer."

"Well, we had some help. But my mom says the same thing. She's even talking about buying a place of her own and redoing it." He paused and then sat beside her. "She loves coming over here."

"She's terrific. She has so many ideas for the house. We were talking about the bedrooms upstairs, and the library..." She didn't speak for a few seconds. "It's meant a lot to me, to spend time with your mother and Dinah. To feel..." She paused again. "...like I belong here."

"They both think you're great."

Summer reached over and laid a hand on his arm. "And you," she added. "I like spending time with you." She left her hand there for a moment, and he laid his own on top of it, gently, as if with too much pressure he might burst the bubble they hovered inside.

He swallowed. "What about Gabe?"

"What about him?"

"You get things sorted out?"

She nodded, not really sure how to answer. "I think so."

"I hope so." He laced his fingers through hers and didn't speak again.

"Think you'll ever build your own place?" Summer asked

185

after a few moments of silence. "You're good at it."

He smiled. "I don't think I'll build from scratch. I'd like to restore one, maybe. Do something like this." He flushed. Even in the half-light Summer could see it, a darkening of the cheeks, a shine in the center of his eyes. "Well, not exactly like this. Something on a smaller scale."

"I know what you mean."

Summer thought she heard something scuttling in the shadows behind her—a mouse? a squirrel looking for a spot to bed down?—and she turned to look over her shoulder. A bulky outline in the darkness startled her. It looked almost like a person, and she jumped.

"Is that—is that a guitar?"

He followed her gaze. "Oh, yeah. I was playing a little for Dinah, earlier."

"I didn't know you were the musical type." It seemed like a silly thing to say—after all, what did she know about him? A few puzzle pieces, a story here and there, not enough to put together the whole, complex person Damian Knight seemed to be. "Would you play something for me?" She didn't know where the request came from and was surprised when it left her lips.

"Sure." He moved past her, and the warmth from his sleeve touched her bare arm. She shivered in the hot night air.

Damian took the instrument from its case and cradled it in careful arms. Tuning, tweaking, he strummed a few chords and began to play "Yesterday" by the Beatles. At first it was only instrumental melody, the strings of the guitar humming the poignant song. But after a minute he began to sing along. His voice was husky but certain, caressing the words as if he'd sung them a hundred times.

Summer leaned against the railing and watched him. The strong, thick fingers that usually wound themselves around a

186

hammer now danced across the strings. The forehead that frowned all day in concentration smoothed. Damian sang, and when the song was over he played "Take It Easy" by the Eagles and sang again.

After the final chord he stopped. The music echoed across the grass, to the hills and back, and Summer let out a breath she didn't know she'd been holding.

"You're good." No one had ever sung to her before. Nerves along her spine stretched and splintered. Her heart, over-full with the night and the music and the man beside her, began a jig.

Damian cleared his throat. "I'm not that good."

"Are you kidding? You're amazing. Do you ever write anything of your own?"

He turned toward her. The movement pressed his thigh against hers, and she thought for a minute he might kiss her. His gaze moved to her mouth and then to the place where the white skin of her breast met the vee of her sundress.

"Yes," Damian said, his breath warm on her cheek. "Sometimes I write my own songs."

He repositioned the instrument, curved his fingers into place and began to play. The melody was simple, a sweet tune that rose and fell without lyrics. It reminded Summer of a butterfly in the morning or dawn above the ocean. The notes dropped honey-like into an endless pool of longing. In the middle, it changed, became low and sensual with guttural chords that hovered and hung in the air. Damian's shoulders hunched, and his arms tightened with intensity as he played on. A pause, and then the first melody returned, sweeter than the start, if that was possible. The sun coming out after a brilliant summer storm. A baby waking with a smile to a brand new day. It faded, grew, then faded again to nothing. With the final chord, the notes vanished into the night.

"God, that was..." Summer couldn't find the words. "...beautiful," she finished, but it wasn't enough to describe the passion or the complexity of the song.

He smiled. "Thanks."

"Does it have a title?"

He looked toward her and paused, opened his mouth and closed it again. "Summer's Song."

Damian set down the guitar and moved toward her, and this time Summer saw the kiss coming. She felt it, knew it and wanted it with every part of her. He brushed his lips against hers, reached up with one hand to cup her cheek, and the step fell away beneath her. Sweet lightness flooded her stomach, her chest, her mouth. He pulled away, whispered her name, pressed his cheek to her temple and let her feel the pulse that raced there.

"Summer." The name sighed out of him, and he kissed her again.

Her fingers reached for him, felt the smooth, strong muscles of his chest and drew him close. Kisses moved along her cheek, her chin, down to her collarbone, until she moaned with a pleasure she couldn't remember ever feeling before. One hand stroked the curve of her breast, and she shivered. Burying her fingers in his hair, she pulled Damian to her. Lips parted and tongues searched, until she could hardly tell where she ended and he began.

The days flipped backwards. She had come here wanting nothing, expecting nothing. Yet something—everything—had changed. First the house. Then dark memories. Then days of light and laughter, of Dinah and Hannah, of Rachael and Cat, strung together like stones on a string. Summer had never believed she might call Pine Point home again. Yet here she sat, wanting Damian Knight's touch, his kiss, his songs, more than she remembered wanting anything in her life. Maybe coming home didn't mean going backwards, after all. Maybe it meant growing up, making new discoveries, learning to forgive the past and finding that the future held myriad possibilities.

Her heart swelled as she took Damian by the hand and led him inside.

Summer moved under him in waves. Silent. Powerful. Damian pressed his lips to the expanse of her neck and the smooth skin there to keep himself from uttering words that made no sense. Her hips arched toward him and when he looked down, he felt himself slipping into the inky pools of her eyes.

"Damian." It was an urgent whisper.

He lifted himself away from her slightly, missing the contact of skin against skin at once.

"What?"

She shook her head, and he knew it wasn't his name she was speaking at all, but a word to hold onto, a handful of syllables to ground herself before she gave into the pleasure entirely. Through the curtainless windows, moonlight streaked the sheets, the floor, the curve of her shoulder. He ran his fingertips from her chin to her waist and watched her shudder. He loved it. He wanted to make her move like that all night long.

So many years it had been. Forever, really, since Damian had wanted a woman the way he wanted Summer Thompson in that moment.

She clutched at his back, her eyes dark with passion, and he surrendered. To lose himself inside her would be the sweetest way to end this day. To end every day. He met her tongue with his, drank her in, tasted wine and chocolate and

Allie Boniface

the tinge of want beneath it all.

He had to stop. For a few moments, he wanted to prolong the pull of desire that stretched along his limbs. And he wanted to prolong hers.

He rolled away from her and slid into the sheets. She looked at him in wonder. He pressed one finger against her lips. Outside, an owl sounded a long, haunted hoot. She smiled, and the movement of her mouth against his hand nearly undid him. He swept the hair from her forehead and studied the scars along her temple, reminders of the accident that had torn her life apart.

Pain, he sensed, still coursed through her veins. It hung around her eyes and turned down the corners of her mouth from time to time. When she looked at the cemetery gates. When she talked to Rachael sometimes. But there was none of that now, and he imagined there was no worry on his face as well. For once. She ran her fingers over his jaw, catching on the rough stubble, and all he saw in her gaze was want.

Second by second, he slipped down the length of her. He moved from her neck to the smooth skin in the center of her chest, to her navel. She reached for him. Pressing her hands to the sheet, he moved again. To the ridge of her hipbone. To the crease between belly and long, slender thigh. To the damp curls of hair that parted her legs. Then lower, until his tongue met velvet, and he could have stayed there all night long, just tasting her.

She called out his name as she came.

Chapter Eighteen

When Summer woke, the moon had crested in the blue-black sky. She rolled over and reached for Damian. Nothing but empty sheets. Her heart thudded against her breastbone and she sat up suddenly. Something had woken her. A car driving by? An animal rummaging in the bushes? She pulled the sheet to her shoulders, chilled despite the humid night air. She still wasn't used to sleeping in the countryside. The sounds and the heaviness of silence after sundown were so different from San Francisco. She closed her eyes, thankful for the bed beneath her and the man who'd helped her christen it. A glorious warmth still clung to the curves of her skin, and she could feel his hands and his mouth moving over her. Inside her.

The bathroom door clicked open. She opened one eye and tried to think of a clever comment, a teasing remark. But all she really wanted to do was tell Damian to hurry back because she wanted him next to her again.

"Hey." A crack of light glimmered across the floor. "You okay?"

"Bad dream, I guess."

"I know. You were moving around a lot."

"I was?" She tried to catch the fragments of dream still slipping around her head. She couldn't.

"And talking." He slid back under the sheets. When he

reached for her, she shivered. *Again,* she thought. *I could do that again. Every night.*

"You kept saying 'No'." He nuzzled her ear. "I was hoping you weren't talking about me."

"Never."

He stopped kissing her and sat up. "What was that?"

"What was what?"

"Thought I heard something."

She looked outside. "Yeah, me too. The wind, maybe. Or ghosts."

"You think this place is haunted?"

"No. I was kidding." She ran her fingers along his arm. "I think we're all haunted, in some way."

He didn't relax. "I wonder if—" He pulled his watch from the pocket of his shorts, tossed on the floor. "I should go home."

"It's two in the morning."

"I know, but..."

"They're fine." She whispered the words along his chest and let her hands drift below the sheet.

"I guess." He bent his head to catch her mouth again, and she looped one leg over his. Her skin burned in all the places he touched it.

ᏸ

Close to dawn, a cell phone rang.

Summer reached in the direction of the bed stand. She still wasn't used to having furniture in this room. Heck, she wasn't used to this room, period. Damian's hand drifted over her thigh, and she smiled.

"It's mine," he said. "Hello? What? Mom, wait—" Panic filled his voice. "How?" He sat up and threw off the sheet. "What did he say? Are the police there? All right, I'm coming home right now."

"What is it? What happened?" Dread froze Summer to the bed. She couldn't move. She could only stare as Damian pulled on his clothes. His shirt ended up inside out.

"T.J. was at the house. Sonofabitch!" His voice shook. "He took Dinah."

"Wait—what? How?"

"I told you." He grabbed his shoes and headed for the front door. She still hadn't managed to crawl to her feet or find her clothes. "I told you I heard something last night. He was probably sneaking around—" His voice broke. "I told you I needed to be at home with them." He punched the doorframe. "I never should have stayed here."

The words sliced through her, white-hot.

"But how—I don't understand how he found them. I thought you said he was..."

Damian didn't answer. Her stomach turned over, wanting him, wanting to help him, not knowing how.

"Let me do something." She found a T-shirt and shorts and pulled them on with shaking hands. "Let me come with you." She reached for Damian's arm, but he pulled away as if she'd burned him.

"Goddamn Theo James Braxton." He blued the air with curses. "I'll fuckin' kill you when I find you. I swear to God."

"Wait—what did you—"

"I knew it," he said, his breath coming in pants. "I knew—I should have left—I should have gone home." He turned, long enough for her to see the emotion splashed across his face.

193

"You said it was nothing. You told me to stay." He pulled open the door.

"Did you say Theo James...?" Something clicked inside Summer's head. Nausea washed over her.

You know the way to County Route 78?

I'm lookin' for an address. Old buddy of mine.

Name's Theo.

"Is he—" Oh God, she didn't want to ask. "He isn't...six feet or so, muscular, greasy dark hair? Grayish eyes?"

Damian stared at her. "Yeah." His voice was flat. "Why?"

"He was downtown yesterday. Outside Flo's." Suddenly she felt like Alice in a black, black wonderland, with everything she thought she knew turned upside down. "He asked me for directions, and I..."

Damian froze. Still as stone, his mouth twisted in anguish, he waited as she stammered on.

"I didn't—oh, God..." What had she done?

"You told him where we live?" His eyes changed from sky blue to almost black.

"No, I—he said he was looking for a friend." Repeating Theo's explanation out loud sounded even more ridiculous than she could have imagined. "I didn't know who he was." Damian couldn't be blaming her for this. Could he? "Let me come with you. Let me help."

"Don't bother." His face was as empty as his voice. "You've done enough."

He paused for an awful second at the bottom of the porch steps, and then he broke into a run, heading through the trees toward the farmhouse as fast as he could. He didn't look back.

⋙⋘

Summer crept back to the bedroom, stunned. Minutes passed. Maybe hours. She bent at the waist and dry-heaved. She could barely process what had just happened. Her vision blurred as the room wheeled around her. *Dinah—gone. Hannah—betrayed. Damian—furious, and with good reason.*

"My God." She dropped her head into her hands. Yesterday, brilliant and cloudless, had begun like any other. How had it wound its way to this ending? She curled into a ball on the bed and let the tears drip between her knees. T.J., or Theo, or whatever his stupid name was, had taken Dinah. He'd broken into the farmhouse, into all of their lives, and ripped away a child. And she'd given him directions to the front door. Then told Damian not to worry when he heard a noise in the middle of the night. Her heart ached, and she thought she might throw up. *It's my fault.* She crawled to the bathroom and hung her head over the toilet bowl.

"Do you like my brother?" Dinah's cricket voice echoed in her head.

"How much do you like Gabe?" Donnie used to ask her. *"Do you like him? Or really, really like him?"*

Summer wept harder. They sounded so much alike, more than she'd ever realized.

She pressed her fingertips against her eyelids. Again she saw Donnie in the back seat of the car. Then Dinah dancing in the circle under the oak trees. Donnie teasing her with a garter snake. Dinah handing her a bouquet of flowers. Their two voices whispered inside her head, over and over again, until another voice rose above them and the memory shifted yet again.

"Let me drive. Please?"

"No. You can't. I will."

"But you've been drinking."

"Only one beer. Maybe two."

He laughed, and in that moment she thought she'd probably let him do whatever he wanted.

"No, I'll drive."

"You'll get in trouble."

"It's only five miles. And it's clear. See? Full moon. Lots of stars."

He kissed her, right there, in front of her brother, until Donnie made gagging noises and pleaded for them to stop. Summer didn't care. She wanted to kiss Gabe—love him, breathe him in—for the rest of the night.

"Let's go."

"Okay. But be careful."

"I will..."

Summer sat up and pressed her hands to the tile floor to stop them from shaking. She'd never remembered that part. Never. Her mind had always stuck on the minutes just before and after the accident. It had never rewound far enough for her to see earlier in the night.

Until now.

Now—oh, God—now she remembered everything about the accident. Everything about the crash, Donnie's death, the whole amazing loss of that night—and it wasn't Gabe's fault at all.

"It was mine."

C3♥

Damian ran down the path as fast as he could. He gagged and a single string of saliva escaped his lips. Somehow, he wished he could drop to his knees and be sick as a dog to rid the terrible feeling in his stomach. *T.J. found us. He took Dinah. It's my fault.*

Like a rhythm, the words beat a terrible staccato against his skull. In the half-light of dawn, shadows surrounded him. A branch caught him across the cheek, drawing blood, but he barely noticed. Moments later, he burst from the trees where the path met the stone driveway of the farmhouse. An officer stood on the porch, one hand on his holster.

"Whoa! Hold it right there." He drew his gun.

Damian froze, hands in the air. Gravel sprayed around him as he slid to a stop. "I'm—" For a minute, he couldn't catch his breath. "Damian Knight. Hannah's son. Dinah's my sister."

The officer eyed him but kept his hand on his gun. "Lemme see some ID."

Damian reached for his wallet with shaking fingers. It fell to the ground. "Shit." He scooped it up and pulled out a dog-eared license. He stayed where he was and held it out.

"Slowly." The officer beckoned Damian forward.

Damian climbed the steps. "Please. You gotta tell me what's going on with my sister."

The officer took an eternity reading his license before handing it back. "I'm Officer Burdick." He shook Damian's hand in introduction and with the other pushed the door open behind him. "My partner's inside taking your mother's statement."

"How is she?"

"Holding up."

"And Dinah?" He almost couldn't ask, didn't want to hear the response.

"We've issued an Amber Alert and closed the roads out of town."

"Mom?" Damian barreled down the hallway. Every lamp in the house burned, filling the small rooms with brash, unnatural light. In the living room, an end table lay on its side with magazines scattered across the carpet. Broken glass crunched under his feet.

Jesus Christ. The last six years, all he'd worried about was this, T.J. tracing them to New York, to Pine Point, and hurting his mother and sister. He'd been so careful. He'd locked the doors and lain awake at night tense with listening. He'd warned his mother again and again. Yet somehow, T.J. had broken through the cracks of their life anyway.

Hannah sat at the kitchen table with another police officer opposite her. He looked to be twenty-five at the most, and Damian wondered what kind of experience the kid had. Writing a few traffic tickets? Checking for underage drinkers at the town bars? Pulling a drunken husband off his wife? He couldn't imagine anyone in Pine Point was equipped to deal with a kidnapping. He sure as hell wasn't.

The baby-faced kid with the dark blond crew cut stood and offered his hand. He spoke in the same clipped tone as his partner on the porch. "Mornin', sir. My name's Officer Wallace."

Damian didn't answer. "Are you okay?" He hugged Hannah's thin shoulders and tried to stop them from shaking.

She remained silent. A crumpled tissue in her hands twirled around and around her fingers until it shredded and fell to her lap. Her left cheek, red and swollen, was beginning to purple. Tears tracked a path to her chin and dripped off onto the table.

Damian forced himself to pull open a drawer and find a frayed towel. He dumped some ice cubes into it and wrapped it closed at both ends, the way he had so many times in the past. *Sick. I'm going to be sick.* "Mom?" Frightened, he leaned down and stared into the depths of her gaze. He held the towel to her bruised cheek and stroked the back of her hair with one hand.

"Mom? I'm right here."

After a long minute, Hannah blinked, and her eyes readjusted to the light. Her head leaned into his touch, seeking comfort. Pupils swelled and saw him. "Damian." The word fell from her mouth and bounced onto the floor, void of expression. With an unsteady hand, she reached up and took the makeshift ice pack from him.

"She hasn't said too much since we arrived," Officer Wallace began, "but she was able to give me a brief statement." He flipped the pages of a small spiral notebook. "She was in the kitchen making breakfast, heard something out back of the house..." He frowned at the notepad. "When she looked out the window, she saw the suspect. She attempted to secure the door—"

"It was unlocked?" How many times had he told his mother to keep the deadbolt fastened? Not that it mattered. T.J. could have broken it off with one hand.

"I'm not sure if it was locked or not," the officer answered in a neutral tone.

Not judging, Damian thought, just doing his job. Gathering and reporting the facts.

The man kept his face down and continued to read. "She attempted to secure the door, but the intruder forced it open before she could. He threatened to hurt her if she didn't tell him where Dinah was, and when she didn't—"

Good girl.

"—he pushed her out of the way and went through the house looking for the girl. Did some damage in the living room

199

and hallway—"

"I saw."

Officer Wallace cleared his throat. "He found Dinah upstairs in her bedroom and carried her out to the car. According to your mother, she appeared to be a little confused but not frightened. Happened approximately..." he looked at his watch, "...forty-five minutes ago." He closed the notepad.

Tears continued to drip down his mother's face, and every so often she raised a hand to wipe them. Under the kitchen lights, the moisture on her fingernails gleamed, like an odd manicure painted by grief.

"I'm sorry." She pressed the towel to her cheek with a weary hand.

"Don't you dare apologize. You didn't do anything wrong. It's not your fault." *It's mine. I wasn't here to stop him.* Enraged, guilty, helpless with grief, he wanted to cut his own throat, tear out his hair, run to the roof and jump off into blackness, as if the pain would somehow bring back his sister and punish him for his negligence all at once. He couldn't believe he'd been careless enough to spend the night at Summer's.

Again he heard her confession that she'd given T.J. directions. It took all his strength not to punch the nearest solid surface. *I trusted her.* Okay, maybe she hadn't known who T.J. was. But shouldn't she have suspected something? Where the hell was woman's intuition at a time like that?

"What are we doing?" he demanded. "What can I do?"

The cop rested his hands on an ample belly. "Got two patrol cars out in town now. We've notified every department between here and Albany to the east, Syracuse to the west." He cleared his throat. "If you can find a recent picture of your sister, that would help. Not much else you can do except wait."

Damian found some extra copies of Dinah's school picture

and handed three to the officer. Then he trudged to the sink and splashed water on his face. His fists opened and closed. Staring out the window, he pictured T.J. there, waiting in the shadows of the lawn, creeping around the house to find the weak spot. Like a fox sniffing out his prey. He brought a hand close to his mouth and then retched. His mother turned away, and the cop cleared his throat. Damian retched again, turned on the water to rinse it away and wept.

Ten minutes passed. Twenty. He paced around the first floor like a jaguar. Restless. Angry. Needing out. Hannah picked up a sponge and circled it over the kitchen counter in a sweeping motion, again and again, her eyes somewhere beyond the house.

The three of them waited, silent, as the minutes marched by. The clock on the stove read six fifty. Six fifty-five. Seven o'clock. Hannah returned to her seat at the table. Damian continued to pace, cracking his knuckles and staring from the refrigerator to the countertops to his mother and back again. The policeman's radio crackled with static.

Suddenly the cop who'd been watching the front door strode into the room. "We have a lead."

Hannah rose with a start, the napkin shredded to soggy confetti in her lap. "Tell me," she said, her voice clear and steady. Her fingers pinched the table and she swayed on her feet. "Tell me you found my daughter."

Damian fought to keep his heart from leaping out of his chest. *No bad news*, it thudded. *No bad news. If he's done something to Dinah, I'll rip every limb from his body.*

"Apparently the kidnapper called the police station a few minutes ago. Says he wants guaranteed full custody of the girl." He cleared his throat. "We weren't able to get a trace on the call. But ah—right now he's considered armed and dangerous. From what he said, there's a possibility he has a weapon of some sort."

Hannah's face lost all color. "He has a gun?"

"We don't know that," Officer Burdick responded. "Ma'am, we have our best negotiator waiting for him to call back. Odds are, if your ex-husband really wants custody of his daughter, he's not gonna do anything to hurt her."

"But you don't know that for sure," Damian said. Fear choked him. He knew T.J. better than these men did. He knew what the bastard was capable of.

"No," the policeman said. "We don't."

Chapter Nineteen

"Did you hear about Dinah?" Summer closed the ambulance corps' break room door. She'd come straight here as soon as the sun crested the hills, unable to think of anything else. When she walked in the front entrance, the kid sitting behind the desk simply pointed to where Gabe waited in the back.

He nodded. "A few minutes ago, on the scanner. I'm sorry."

She rubbed away more tears. "How can this happen? Here in Pine Point—how?"

"I don't know." He sat on the arm of a chair and cracked his knuckles. Neither of them spoke for a few minutes. "Is that why you came? To see if I could help? I don't know if I can. I mean, I'll try, see if maybe—"

"No." She shook her head. "I w-wanted to tell you—that I remembered. Just this morning." She drew in a deep breath. "I remember what happened the night my brother died." She looked straight at him. "You lied."

Gabe said nothing.

"You told them you were driving the night of the accident."

He waited an eternity before answering. "Yes."

"But why?" She could barely breathe. "Why would you do that?"

He sank onto the couch in the center of the room. "It's hard to explain."

After a minute, she sat beside him. Her fingers brushed his. "You let me drive because you were drinking. And because I wanted to."

His chin dipped in acknowledgement.

"I didn't have a license." She recalled the arguments with her father over that. *Too dangerous*, he'd say. *You don't need to learn. Not until you're eighteen. I'll take you wherever you need to go.*

She said the next words quietly, piecing them together as she went, unearthing her own history though it pained her with every breath. "You were at a party. At the Hadleys'."

"Only until you got off work."

"I know." She'd never suspected Gabe of cheating on her, and she didn't now. "We didn't go to the drive-in?" That was the only part that remained fuzzy.

"We did, but it was crowded. So we left. It was late, anyway, and Donnie was supposed to be home—"

Summer pressed her hand on top of his. She remembered the rest. Taking the keys from Gabe when she smelled beer on his breath. Insisting she drive his car. Thinking the few times her father had let her practice were enough.

But with her teenage crush beside her, the warmth and excitement of the night and the bright headlights at the intersection—it had all confused and distracted her. "I should have stopped." There wasn't a sign in her direction, just a flashing yellow light, but she should have stopped anyway. She should have known; it was a dangerous crossing, and people blew through it all the time.

"Oh, God. Wait—what's—why isn't that car stopping? Gabe?"

Her foot moved from the gas pedal to the brake, but not in time. A flash in the rearview mirror, her brother's pale face, flew across the periphery of her vision. Exploding metal. Screaming tires. An impact that shook every tooth in her head.

Then nothing at all.

"How could you tell them that?" She sobbed. "Why?"

"It wasn't your fault."

She let herself lean against him and bear the weight of her head and shoulders. Her eyes closed, and she began to shake with silent sobs. *Of course it was.*

Gabe put an arm around her. "Summer, Mr. Hartwell ran the red in the other direction. He had a stop. You had a yield. Plus he'd been drinking, was bombed out of his mind. Everyone knew that."

She couldn't answer. *That was why we rushed to get out of the car.* Gabe hadn't wanted anyone to see that she was driving. She, the one without a license. She'd been at the wheel the night her brother died. Not Gabe. Pinpricks of light behind her eyes turned to black.

"Son, come over here, please. Just have a couple of questions to ask you..."

As the cop turned his back, Gabe peeled her fingers open and pried the car keys from Summer's sweaty palm.

"B-but...you went to jail for me."

Gabe sighed, and for the first time, she heard sadness in his voice. "Well, I thought Hartwell was gonna make it. Thought they'd charge him. I never guessed..."

"That they'd charge you instead?"

She felt him nod against her cheek. With one arm around her, he sat motionless.

"Why didn't you just tell them the truth?" She whispered the words into his shirtfront.

He didn't have to answer. She could tell by the pulse in the hand that touched her cheek, and in the way his chest heaved with the weight of the last ten years.

"It was the right thing to do, Summer," Gabe said after a long time. His voice was rough. "Your dad—he lost his son that night. I didn't want him to lose his daughter too."

CʒꝸꙅO

Summer sat on a stone bench in the town park long after Gabe had left for a call in Silver Valley.

"I didn't want him to lose his daughter too..."

His daughter. Like Dinah. Summer pressed one hand against her mouth. What if another child was about to die in Pine Point? They hadn't heard anything in the hour she'd stayed at the ambulance corps. No news of Dinah, good or bad, had crackled over the police scanner.

The bench bit into the backs of her legs. An ant crawled over her toe and continued on to climb a blade of grass. She didn't move. If she did, she thought she might break. She couldn't go back to the house. She could barely remain upright. The sun burned the back of her neck, but she didn't care. She was surprised she could still feel anything at all. A horn beeped somewhere over on Main Street. She didn't look up. Instead she studied the veins on the backs of her hands and the blood that ran through them.

So much blood that night...

Now that she'd cracked open that part of her memory, it seemed the details wouldn't stop coming. Her brother's Yankees hat sitting astride the double line in the road. The police sirens screaming in her ears. The tears that wet her shirtfront. A single stoplight flashing red one way, yellow the other, in a macabre smear of color that lit up the sky. The blood on her hands and Gabe's face, the shattered glass sprayed everywhere she looked.

How did I forget?

She turned her hands slightly and watched the shadows they cast on the pavement. It was funny, the way the mind worked. If she hadn't forgotten, she probably would have gone mad.

It wasn't your fault.

Her head swung back and forth as she silently answered Gabe's reassurance. It was, of course. Gabe might not have avoided the accident if he'd been driving, but then again, he might have. He would certainly have slowed at the yellow light. And he might have paid better attention. He might have seen the other car, braked sooner, or swerved into the safety of the shoulder. Or he might not have.

The historian in her whispered something else. *You can study every last detail,* her favorite college professor had told a full lecture hall. *You can put all the pieces of an artifact back together. You can match up all the edges, mend the lines until they become invisible, but you still won't know it all. You will never be able to step back with both feet to that moment of creation and truly relive it. We can only work with the knowledge we have now. We can only imagine.*

And so, Summer had made a life out of imagining. She'd spent hours putting together the pieces of other people's lives.

She'd become fascinated with unearthing clues and determined to write stories that would decipher them. She lived the museum, loved it, made it the career that consumed her. Until now. Until she was faced with her own pieces. Unlike all the rest of history, she didn't have to conjure any part of this story; she knew it front to back and beginning to end.

After a long time, she opened her eyes. Every part of her felt as though it weighed a hundred pounds—her head, her eyelids, her hands, and her feet when she tried to make them work. It took her two tries to remain standing.

She might have ruined her relationship with Damian, she might have endangered Dinah's welfare, but one thing was simple enough: she couldn't let the residents of Pine Point go on thinking Gabe had killed her brother. She had to make that right, anyway.

ඥෑ

Summer walked the half-mile from the ambulance corps to downtown Pine Point. Zeb's Diner had been a fixture on Main Street for as long as she could remember, and as she crossed to it, she gazed with nostalgia at its red-and-white striped awnings. How many heartaches had she and Rachael nursed here? How much gossip had they shared? She hadn't stepped foot inside the place for ten years, yet the jukebox sat against the same wall, and the brightly lit menu hung above the same shiny counter. Even the color scheme remained identical—turquoise leatherette booths with silver chrome molding and a black-and-white checkerboard floor. Old photos of 1920s celebrities hung at crooked angles on the wall.

She met Rachael at a back booth and spilled the entire story in a matter of minutes. "...and so thanks for coming."

Rachael fished a stack of napkins from the dented dispenser and handed them over. "My dad told me," she said as Summer started to cry. "He's got the scanner turned on. Police from here to Silver Valley have all the roads blocked. They'll find the guy."

Summer blew her nose. "What if they don't?"

"Don't say that. They *will*."

She reached for a menu. She wasn't hungry, but she needed to distract herself. And she needed something to hold onto.

"I know you're upset," Rachael said around her straw, "but it's not like it's your fault. The guy sounds like a total psycho."

Summer choked. "Actually, I think it might be. My fault, I mean."

The straw dropped from Rachael's mouth. "What do you mean? How?"

"I gave him directions to their house."

"What?"

She told the story as quickly as she could.

"Stop it," Rachael said before she had finished. She shook her head. "You told him how to get to County Route 78? That's it? That's what you're beating yourself up about?"

Summer didn't know what to say. *Of course.*

Rachael handed her some more napkins. "Big deal. You know how long that road is? How many people live on it? You didn't know who he was or who he was looking for."

"But I should have."

"Why?" Rachael dismissed her with a wave of one hand. "You're being ridiculous. It wasn't your fault. If you didn't give him directions, the next person to come along would have. You know that. And if not last night, he would have taken her another time."

"Maybe." Summer still couldn't shake the guilt or the accusing look on Damian's face as he stormed away. She took a deep breath. "But that isn't the only thing."

Rachael frowned and waited for her to go on.

She squared her shoulders and laced her fingers together. "Remember how I told you I could never remember what happened the night Donnie died?"

"Yeah. What does that have to do with anything?"

She pressed her fingertips to her lips and fought for composure. She'd have to tell this story more than once. People needed to know, starting with her best friend. *Get it over with. The first time will be the hardest.* "This morning, I remembered. I was driving. The night Donnie died, I was driving Gabe's car."

"Wait—what?" Rachael stared at her. "But you didn't have your license."

"Exactly."

Rachael sat back in the booth. "I can't believe it. You're wrong. You have to be."

"I'm not, Rach. I think maybe with what happened with Dinah—it triggered it or something. I was thinking about her, and about Donnie, and then...I just remembered everything. I was driving because Gabe had been at a party earlier that night. He'd been drinking." She gulped. "So I thought it would be better if I drove us home. Safer."

"He went to jail," Rachael whispered.

"I know." Tears covered her face. "But why didn't anyone tell me that? Why didn't you?" Maybe she would have remembered sooner, or been able to change the outcome of the sentencing. Frustration and guilt seeped into her pores. She'd never be able to give those two years back to Gabe. Never.

Rachael rested her chin on one palm. "We didn't talk for—what? Almost a year after you left. And when we did, you were so...fragile. Confused. I didn't know what you knew and what you didn't. All you talked about was college or your latest job. Never anything about the accident or your brother. And definitely never anything about Gabe."

"I didn't know where to start."

"And now? What the hell are you gonna do now?"

She met her best friend's gaze. "I have to tell people. They have to know the truth. I was driving, and I didn't see the other car, and I was the one who didn't stop in time. Not him."

"Oh, Summer." Rachael got up and slid into the booth beside her. She folded her friend in a hug, and they sat there a long time without speaking.

It is these small pieces that heal. The pieces you dig up, dust off and show to the light, hoping they'll hold their form without shattering. One at a time. She closed her eyes and wept into Rachael's shoulder.

"I want to go on Channel 6. As soon as I can."

Rachael pulled back with a look of horror. "Are you kidding? You don't have to announce it to the world."

But she'd made up her mind. The only thing she needed to do was call the local cable station and find out when she could get airtime.

Chapter Twenty

Ginny Jameson, Channel 6 anchor, arranged her face and fluffed her hair. Summer stood across from her, frozen. The clock in the center of town chimed six times.

"I still can't believe you're doing this," Rachael whispered from behind her left shoulder. "You don't have to."

Yes, I do. Summer looked out at the knot of people that had gathered near the steps of the Pine Point Central School. She was still startled it had happened so quickly. One call to the police, another to the central desk at the cable station, and a camera-and-lighting entourage hovered around them, ready for the evening news.

"Good evening. This is Ginny Jameson for Channel 6 News, coming to you live from Pine Point, where a startling turn of events has stirred up this small town."

To say the least. Summer wound her fingers in her skirt and hoped she didn't have to move. If she did, she'd catch a heel in the stairs and sprawl out for the entire viewing area to see. She squinted against the camera lights. She thought she saw Gabe standing at the edge of the crowd. She hadn't told him about the news conference, but she was pretty sure Pine Point's grapevine still worked as well as ever.

"Earlier today, eight-year old Dinah Knight was kidnapped from her home by her estranged father..."

Summer fought against tears. *Don't listen. Just figure out what you're going to say.* She could only deal with one tragedy at a time. Better not to think about Dinah, or Hannah and T.J., until later, when they were off camera. And better not to think of Damian at all. Ginny widened her eyes as she told the story of abduction, stringing together scant details. "...authorities have widened their search, but there have been no leads since early this morning."

A movement at the edge of the crowd made Summer turn. Damian eased his way past the steps and behind a cameraman. The blood left her face. She hadn't expected him to come.

"...anyone with information about a man resembling Theodore Braxton or a red pickup truck with Maryland plates, should contact authorities at once."

They cut to a commercial, and a woman darted in to powder Ginny's nose. Summer smoothed the hair at her temples and blew out a breath. She could do this. She had to. She looked across the tops of people's heads, searching for Damian, but he'd disappeared.

"All set?" Ginny asked with a bright smile.

Summer nodded. The cameraman adjusted his light, and then she couldn't see anyone in the crowd. *Just as well.*

"We're back in Pine Point, where a little girl was taken hostage early this morning." Ginny began her recap in a somber tone. Her smile of thirty seconds earlier had vanished. "But that isn't the only cloud hanging over this town tonight, where friends and neighbors wait and pray for Dinah Knight's safe return."

The newscaster paused and turned to face Summer. "Ten years ago, another youth disappeared, this one the victim of a deadly car accident. A local man served two years for manslaughter in the case, but today, the sister of the boy came forward to claim responsibility for the accident."

Ginny thrust her microphone in front of Summer. "Is it true that you were driving the car the night your brother died?"

The voices around her swelled with surprise. Whispers turned into murmurs and became a chaos of chatter. Summer couldn't see the residents of Pine Point, but she knew they stood there gaping at her.

"Yes." She lifted her chin. "I was with Gabe Roberts, but I was driving his car. We were dating at the time. I went into shock right after the accident, and I didn't remember anything for years. Until just a few hours ago, really. But..."

She said the rest as quickly as she could. Don't blame him anymore, she begged the town. It was never his fault. Only once did she try and focus on the faces around her. She thought she saw Gabe with a restless smile on his face that disappeared when someone moved in and clapped a hand on his shoulder. Within minutes, the crowd had obscured him.

"...and I'll be returning to California within the week," she finished. That had been the only easy part of this whole decision. She didn't belong here. She could make amends, but she couldn't carve out a new existence for herself. Just the thought of it exhausted her. Gabe and the town, Damian and his mother and sister—they all would be fine without her.

Ginny wrapped up the segment with another plea for information about Dinah's kidnapping, which Summer echoed. It couldn't happen twice, she thought. This town couldn't lose two children. The universe couldn't be that cold. The setting sun cast shadows across the crowd, but she saw so many faces she knew. Teachers from the school. Tellers from the bank. Neighbors she'd grown up with. Friends she'd turned her back on.

She stumbled down the stairs as the news crew packed up

their vans and headed over the hill to Cedar Crest. No one waited for her, but it didn't matter. She'd done the right thing. Now she needed to do a second right thing. She needed to go back to the police station and see if there was anything she could do to help. Man the call lines. Even make coffee for the cops pulling night duty.

Donnie might have died, but she'd do everything in her goddamned power to make sure Dinah came back home to Pine Point safe and sound.

⋘⋙

He was leaning against the brick wall of the high school, half-hidden by shadows and basketball hoops.

"Hey."

Summer froze.

A car drove by, the lights above them flickered and Gabe materialized a few feet in front of her. "You didn't have to do that."

She hugged herself against a chill. "Yes I did. People needed to know."

"I think most people got over it a while ago." He took a step closer and she could smell his cologne. She didn't recognize it; it wasn't the same stuff he'd worn in high school. *Probably just as well.*

"Doesn't matter. It was still the right thing to do." She edged next to the wall to put a little space between them. The feeling of standing beside him, looking up sideways to catch his grin, tossed her back ten years in a heartbeat.

"Ah, Summer." He met her gaze.

"Have you heard anything about Dinah?"

He shook his head. She checked her cell and wondered if Damian or Hannah would call her. She wondered if she could dare believe she meant that much to them.

Gabe leaned back against the wall. Their shoulders brushed. "You hungry? You want to grab some dinner?"

"I don't think so." She couldn't think about eating. Again she saw Damian's cool gaze move across her, then away, as he listened to her confession. She turned toward Gabe, meaning to ask him something about the accident, but the words died on her lips when she saw the way he was looking at her.

Curious. Familiar. Caring.

A second later he leaned down and kissed her. Her fingers curled around air. She leaned into the kiss for a moment, remembering the dozens of times he'd touched her exactly the same way. Then she pulled back at the same instant he did.

He stuffed his hands into his pockets, and his smile crooked a little. "Not there anymore, is it?"

She shook her head, surprised. She always thought she would hold a piece of her heart for Gabe Roberts forever.

"You love him? This Damian guy?"

She lifted her shoulders. "I don't know."

"You should tell him how you feel."

"Not sure it's really the best time."

"You should tell him anyway." Gabe paused, then leaned over and placed a chaste kiss in the center of her forehead. "There isn't always a best time, or a best way, or a best anything when it comes to stuff like that. But time gets away from you before you know it. It's tough to say things after too long, especially when there's a couple thousand miles between you."

I know.

216

Summer stood there a long time after he left, thinking.

ભ્જજ

Damian stared out the window of Zeb's Diner, where his mother had sent him for coffee after the press conference.

"You can't stay in the house and pace," she'd said. "You'll make me crazy."

Then he saw Summer pull up and park outside the police station, and his throat closed. He was glad when she didn't come into the diner. He didn't know what he'd say to her. He'd watched the whole live news segment over at the school, and though he knew in some way hers was a noble gesture, he couldn't see past the fact that she'd lied all those years ago and let someone else take the blame. So she was leaving town, huh? Maybe he didn't know Summer Thompson at all. Maybe no one did.

He wrapped his hands around a cold cup of coffee and eyed an empty Main Street. As the wind shifted, clouds scudded across the sky. A half-moon glowed down, and from where he sat, he could almost see the end of Main Street, where it turned into Red Barn Road. If he squinted, he could make out the third-floor windows of Summer's house. Dark. Silent and empty. Like he felt right about now.

For the first time all day, thoughts of T.J. and Dinah vanished. He forgot the fear and worry crawling up his skin and lingered over the memory of what had happened at that house less than twenty-four hours earlier. Cream-colored toenails. A hand that rested on his shoulder and a smile that asked him to play for her. A mouth that reached to his, that breathed him in and asked him to stay without saying a word. A naked body beneath his.

My God, she is poetry. She is music under the moon, pieces of a puzzle I want to curl my hands around and move together with my own.

Yet he hadn't said a thing to her. He'd stood there at the school, less than ten yards away, and stared at her without words. He'd wanted to take her in his arms. He'd wanted to blame her. He'd wanted to kiss her. He'd wanted to hate her.

He'd simply wanted her. Still did, more than ever.

Damian shook his head. He couldn't afford to think about her that way. Not now. He checked his watch. Why hadn't they heard anything? His leg jounced with nerves. He couldn't stay here any longer—even staring at the gray walls of the police station was better than watching couples hold hands over milkshakes.

"Damian?"

He looked up. *You gotta be kidding me. Not her. Not tonight.* Before he could say a word, Joyce Hadley slid into the booth beside him.

"I'm so sorry," she whispered.

"What are you doing here?"

She waved toward the front counter, where one of her look-alike sisters was picking up takeout. "Getting dinner." She paused. "I saw you over by the school. While Summer was on the news." Her leg pressed against his. He didn't move away. "I never knew that, about the accident. Guess no one did." She clicked her fingernails on the table. "Can't believe it. Gabe was a good guy. *Is* a good guy."

But Damian didn't want to talk about Gabe Roberts. He'd watched the guy while Summer talked. He'd seen the history on both their faces.

"You haven't heard anything?"

He shook his head. He could smell Joyce's perfume. For some reason, it didn't make him gag tonight. She wore less makeup than usual, and without all that eye goop he could actually see light blue irises surrounded by dark lashes. A picture of Summer lying beside him beneath white sheets circled around his brain and fell away. *She's leaving town. It's too late, anyway.*

He tried to speak but his tongue felt thick, and suddenly Joyce metamorphosed into two faces instead of one. He blinked a few times. Shock, maybe, or delayed fatigue, he thought.

"Have you eaten anything?" Her voice sounded far away.

"No. Can't."

"Let me order you something."

"No. Really. I'll wait 'til we hear something about Dinah."

Joyce reached under the table and took his hand. He let her. "She'll be okay. They'll find her."

But Joyce didn't know that. No one did. "It's my fault." He didn't mean to speak, but somehow the words found their way out.

"What's your fault?"

"That he found us. That he took her. I couldn't protect Mom or Dinah." His knee jiggled. "That's my job, to protect both of them, and I couldn't."

Joyce produced a tissue from somewhere and handed it to him. "You can't have known this would happen. I'm sure he was waiting for the right time, when you weren't there." She ran one finger along his wrist, and loneliness, powerful as a tidal wave, swept over him.

"Let's get some air."

Cฺฬ

Summer stood in the doorway of the Pine Point Police Station. Nothing but shadows and streetlights. Even the sirens were silent. She felt wrung out, exhausted, as if the little life left in her this afternoon had vanished.

"Ah, there's a statute of limitations on involuntary manslaughter," the captain had explained to her a few minutes ago. "Plus, we can't charge someone else with a crime when the first person's already done time for it."

Summer stared straight ahead and realized again the enormity of the sacrifice Gabe had made for her. She could do nothing else to repay him. Nothing to give him back the time he'd lost sitting in a jail cell for something he didn't do. Strangely, the only relief lay in knowing that Pine Point finally knew the truth. Anyone who hadn't watched the six o'clock news would catch the late-night recap in another hour. That person would tell someone down at the gas station, and those people would relate the tale at the beauty parlor or the frozen foods aisle or the hundred other places stories took root. Within a week, everyone living in a fifty-mile radius would know.

She smiled. Knowing that lifted the burden from her shoulders and her heart. The truth, after all, would count for something.

"You okay?" Rachael stood at her elbow.

"Yeah. Thanks for being here."

"I'll come back with you," Rachael offered. "We'll buy ice cream and stay up all night like we used to. If you don't want to be alone, or..."

Summer shook her head. The police had promised to watch the house, and Rachael couldn't help her with the other pain she felt. This was nothing like the grief they'd nursed in grade school. Back then, a cold shoulder from a boy she liked or a rotten grade on a midterm exam warranted two spoons and a carton of chocolate-chip ice cream. Locked away in Rachael's attic bedroom, they'd eat away the sadness until laughter replaced tears. Talking into the early morning, giggling at Cat and his pimple-cheeked friends, Summer had always emerged on the other side of sunrise with a refreshed heart.

But she didn't think anything would give her a second chance with Damian. She'd seen his face at the news conference. "I'll be fine. I just need some sleep."

"You're sure?"

"I'm sure. I'll call you tomorrow."

"You better. First thing."

Summer nodded and waved goodbye. Eyelids heavy with emotion threatened to close before she reached her car. She felt one hundred years old, bent from the strain of a single day. The moment Damian had sung to her and wrapped her in his arms seemed ages gone. She'd had a chance and lost it. That was that, plain and simple. There was no use moping around about it, no use rewinding the day and torturing herself by wondering what she might have done differently.

I need to go home. She slid into her car. *Just bury myself under the covers and find a way to make it through to morning.*

She turned the key in the ignition. A sad, slow blues song filled the car, and she spun the dial to turn it up. Fatigue tightened the back of her neck and she pulled out of the parking space too fast, jerking the wheel and slamming on the brakes as a police car rolled by. She slowed at the blinking red light. A few yards away the neon lights of Zeb's Diner shone against the night sky. Beyond that, nothing but dark, quiet homes. No cars appeared and she was about to press the accelerator and continue the final mile to her house when she saw them.

The girl, petite and blonde, pressed against the man, who leaned at an awkward angle as if he were uncertain about the placement of his feet. Summer stared. Lights and shadows spilled down on them, striping them in yellow and gray, but she would have recognized the couple on the moon. A thin layer of perspiration broke out on her upper lip. Damian and Joyce Hadley stood fifty feet away, arms around each other.

Summer's fingers clenched the steering wheel. Without looking in her direction, they stopped near a thick tree, and even in the dim light, she could see the smile on Joyce's face as she reached up and smoothed the hair from Damian's forehead. Summer bit her lip. She knew how that cowlick dipped down toward his eyes. Every day she watched him push it out of the way while he worked.

Damian's head bent forward. *Oh my god he's going to kiss her.* Summer's breath disappeared. She was suspended in a bubble, trapped inside a terrible theater, forced to watch a horror film she couldn't stop. He was going to kiss Joyce Hadley out on the street for all of Pine Point to see, and Summer was going to have to watch it happen.

She gunned her car and shot through the intersection as fast as she could. Tires squealed, but she didn't care. Less than twenty-four hours after making love to her, Damian was flirting with Joyce in the middle of town. She couldn't believe it.

She coasted to a stop outside her silent house. *I'll stay until they find Dinah. Then I'm gone.* She'd meant every word at the press conference. She would help in whatever way she could. But by the end of the week, she'd be back in San Francisco where she belonged. She squared her shoulders and forced herself to face the truth: Damian had found solace tonight in the local girl, something Summer had stopped being a long time ago. She climbed the back steps and let herself in. The house groaned and settled around her. Dark. Empty. *Sort of like the hole in my chest.*

When her cell phone rang ten minutes later, she'd already slipped into a restless sleep.

Chapter Twenty-One

Theo tried to put weight on his injured hand and failed. Pain shot all the way up to his shoulder. "Fuck."

Using the other hand to bolster himself instead, he made his way off the sagging couch and shuffled across the room. His buddy snored from a mattress in the opposite corner of the old hunting cabin. He crept into the kitchen. This place stunk to high heaven, and he thought something was growing mold inside the refrigerator. Still, he was grateful for a place to hide. The alerts on the radio had him heading for Canada or the New York-Massachusetts border, so he'd stayed put in Wineglass Lake, a tiny town about thirty miles north of Pine Point. Ronny, a dim-witted assistant he'd met on the job last week, hadn't asked questions, just let him crash on the sofa when he showed up a couple of hours ago.

But dammit to hell...Dinah had gotten away from him.

Theo stuck his head under the faucet and slurped. He still couldn't believe it had gone so wrong. He'd planned it all out, waited until he knew Hannah and Dinah would be alone in the house. He hadn't intended to belt his ex-wife, but she'd gotten in the way. Shown more spirit than he remembered. Used to be, she'd let him do whatever he wanted, never gave him any lip. Must be a few years by herself had given her courage. Theo chuckled. He'd put her in her place fast enough, though. After getting Dinah into the car and promising her an ice cream and a puppy later on if she didn't cry, he'd driven west like he planned, taking the back roads and cruising with the lights off whenever he could.

But Dinah had to stop and pee, and when he turned around, she'd taken off. He swore again and ran a wet washcloth over his face. What eight-year-old ran away from her own father? In the middle of the forest edging a no-name town? He'd been lucky to hitch a ride here from some broad with no teeth and a station wagon missing the back bumper. He didn't dare go out and look for Dinah now. He'd run into a pack of local cops within the first ten minutes.

Goddammit, he missed his daughter. He missed watching her sing and dance around the house. Missed having her crawl into his lap and watch television with him after dinner. Hell, he missed having a family, coming home to a warm meal and a soft woman. Didn't look like he'd be having any of that, though, anytime soon.

There was only one person to blame for that. Theo spat into the sink and reached for the bottle of Jack Daniels on the counter.

The way he figured it, Hannah's bastard son had been the cause for every problem in his life since the day he married her and took them both in. Ever since that brat turned old enough to see what went on behind closed doors, he'd been looking out for his mother and sister. Shoving Theo out of the way when all he wanted to do was talk to his wife. Standing between him and his daughter when the girl deserved a spanking. Theo emptied the bottle into his throat. Every damn time he tried to discipline his wife and child, that kid had interfered. To add insult to injury, Damian must have convinced his mother to change their last names back to Knight. As if Braxton wasn't good enough.

"That son of a bitch needs to learn who's boss," Theo muttered, wiping his mouth on a dirty shirtsleeve. "Once and for all." He reached into a kitchen cabinet and pulled out the new bottle he knew Ronny kept there. He stroked the fifth of bourbon with care.

"Come to papa," he whispered and broke the seal. He eased into a stained recliner, propped the bottle between his thighs and checked his watch. Eleven thirty. He took another long drink and turned over possibilities. Forget Hannah and Dinah. This time, he'd go straight to the devil himself. Even with only one good hand, he had no doubt he'd dominate in a fight. Course, having an advantage in the form of a trusty sidearm wouldn't hurt either.

He checked his watch a third time, patted the forty-five lying on the table beside him and watched the moon move across the inky sky.

⁓

Damian stood in the front hallway and watched the cop pace the length of their driveway. Joyce Hadley had left less than an hour ago, after the cops hurried them back to the farmhouse with the news about Dinah. *Call me,* she'd whispered, one damp palm in his, but Damian knew he wouldn't.

The suspect's probably a hundred miles away by now, Officer Burdick had repeated. *We'll call you as soon as we hear anything. We have to focus our efforts now on finding the girl.*

But how do you know he doesn't have her? Doubt had filled Hannah's expression.

Two sets of footprints go in two opposite directions where the truck was ditched. The cop cleared his throat. *He might have gone after her, yes, but it's more likely he's taken off, afraid of getting caught. Typical M.O. with kidnappers when something doesn't go according to plan.*

But then don't you think he'll come back here? Hannah had asked. *Don't you think he'll try to find her again?*

We're keeping a watch on your house. But even a fool doesn't push his luck that much.

The cop's reassurance hadn't convinced Damian. Didn't matter if the police set up a barricade around the farmhouse twenty-four seven for the next three hundred and sixty-five days. If T.J. wanted to, he'd find another way to fracture the safe life the Knights sought. Damian was sure of it.

Hannah sat beside him on the couch. "Listen to me. I want you to go over to the house. Talk to Summer."

"No. Not until we hear something about Dinah."

"Damian." Her voice broke, and she took a deep breath to try to still it. "It might be hours. It might not be 'til morning."

"I don't care. I'm not leaving you here alone."

"You should talk to Summer. You haven't said one word to her since everything happened."

"What am I supposed to say?"

"She cares about Dinah too."

Then she never would have told a stranger how to get to our house. He hadn't told his mother about Summer giving T.J. directions; he couldn't bear to. *And if she cared so much, she would have believed my hunch. She would have listened to me last night when I said I had to leave.* He balled his hands into fists.

"After what she went through today, she needs someone to talk to."

"She lied about driving the night her brother died."

"She did not. She never remembered. And as soon as she did, she stood up and took responsibility." Hannah paused. "Not a lot of people would do that."

He went to the window and pulled back the curtain. "What if something happens while I'm gone?"

"Damian, it's less than a quarter mile from here. The police will tell us the minute they hear anything. And I'll call you."

"I don't know…"

She put a hand on his wrist. "She's leaving. Soon. You heard her say that at the news conference."

"Exactly. So what's the point in talking to her now?" *It doesn't matter. I don't matter. Obviously.*

"Listen to me." Hannah's voice took on an edge "You cannot spend the next fifty years trying to protect me. Or Dinah or yourself. There's a whole life out there, starting with someone on the other side of those trees who's waiting for you to come to your senses. She needs someone tonight. Go see her."

His cheeks warmed.

"Have you even called her?"

He shook his head.

"I don't understand. I see the way you look at her. The way you look at each other." She lifted the house phone from the table beside her. "At least call her and make sure she's all right."

Damian's shoulders sagged. "It's past midnight." Besides, he didn't want to call Summer. He didn't want to stand on the other side of a room and try to make small talk. He wanted to feel her, to kiss her and wind his fingers into her hair. He wanted to play all the songs stored up in his head, the ones that made his fingers itch to play for her. But he didn't know how to begin a conversation after everything that had happened. Plus, he couldn't leave his mother here alone. He wanted to go. He needed to stay. Doing nothing at all trapped him in the middle, where he lost his nerve with every hour that passed.

Chapter Twenty-Two

Summer sat straight up in bed. Something had woken her. Not the sun rising—it wasn't yet dawn. She squinted against the darkness and checked the clock. A little past five. She'd slept barely four hours after tossing and turning and trying to work things out in her head. But despite the little bit of shut-eye, she felt restless and wrung out. She rubbed her eyes. Her cell phone beeped.

A message. That's what had woken her. *Maybe they found Dinah. Oh please please please...* She lunged for the bed stand and fumbled with the tiny keys of her phone. But it was only Rachael.

The time of the garbled message read as twelve-oh-five. "Summer, listen. Dinah... They think Dinah got away from him. Witness said they saw someone matching T.J.'s description walking on a road up past the lake last night. By himself."

Rachael's voice faded out for a moment, replaced by static. "...cops found the guy's truck a little while after that, dumped off at a rest area on the highway."

She got away from him? "So where is she?" Summer asked aloud.

Summer? Where are you? ...Summer?

She pinched the bare skin on her leg and tried to keep from dropping the phone. *This is not then. Dinah is not Donnie.*

"...so the cops are checking the bushes around the rest area and the gas stations close by. They're thinking she slipped out when he stopped somewhere. Maybe a couple of miles away on the other side of the cemetery." Pause. "Just wanted to let you know." Another pause. "Call me when you get this, okay?"

She dropped the phone into her palm. Dinah had gotten away from her father. Thank God. Summer drew her knees up to her chest and hugged them. But what did that mean? Was wandering around lost really any better than being kidnapped? What if the girl fell and hurt herself? What if she—

Summer shook her head to stop the thoughts. Maybe she could help. They must be organizing search parties. She knew this area as well as anyone else who'd grown up here, and much better than Dinah or Damian or Hannah. She played Rachael's message again, trying to draw out any clue of where Dinah might have headed. She frowned. The other side of the cemetery? That wasn't too far from—

A strange noise froze her in place.

"Hello? Mac?" She turned toward the bedroom door, nerves bristling. It was too early for either guy to be showing up for work. *What was that?* She waited another minute, tensed and ready to leap for the nearest window. But she didn't hear it again.

Five thirty, read her digital clock. Summer gave up on sleep and padded out to the kitchen. She turned on the coffeemaker and stared over the treetops to where Damian and Hannah lay sleeping. Or waiting, she supposed. She didn't guess they would have slept a wink.

She filled her mug and walked back through the foyer,

trying not to think of the last time she'd sat on the porch inches away from Damian while he played the guitar and knotted up her insides. Two legs in the darkness, brushing. Her pulse beating too fast. His gaze holding hers as a tune emerged in silver waves beneath his hands. If she closed her eyes, she could almost recapture the melody, the way it moved from his fingers and hung on the air.

Tell him how you feel, Gabe had said. But would she have the chance? Or would it be much smarter to just get on a plane and leave everything behind?

The noise came again. Her heart thudded. She hurried back into her bedroom and checked the bathroom. Nothing. She moved to the window and took a long look at the front yard. Only trees and flowerbeds. She'd almost turned away, convinced her imagination had gotten the best of her, when she saw it—a beat-up sports car parked beyond the hedgerow. Summer squinted. She didn't recognize it.

"Well, look who's here."

The gravelly voice came from her bedroom doorway. She spun around and dropped her mug. Coffee splashed everywhere. A wild-eyed, disheveled man stood ten feet away from her. The man from outside Flo's. *T.J.*

And he was holding a gun.

"Wh-wh—" She tried to form a word and couldn't. Air whistled past her teeth. Her legs gave out and she stumbled, reaching for the window seat.

He took a few steps toward her. "Didn't know anyone was livin' here."

She stared. He smelled terrible—of urine, liquor, body odor and something else. Something evil. She opened her mouth and tried again.

"I'm not lookin' for you," he said, "though this little

predicament might work out to my advantage."

"What are you doing here?" she whispered.

He didn't answer. Instead he let his head fall back, taking in the crown molding, the high ceilings, the chandelier in the foyer behind him. "Nice place."

Summer eyed her cell phone sitting on the bedside table six feet away. It was directly behind the crazy man with the gun.

"Damian do all this?"

"Uh, yeah. And—and Mac."

"Who?" His eyes flashed, bloodshot, and Summer could tell he'd been drinking. She edged closer to the bed.

"You can stay right there." Dropping any pretense of kindness, T.J. stepped closer and pointed the revolver directly at her chest.

Summer's vision fuzzed, and she scrabbled back into the window seat. She eyed the muzzle of the weapon and pressed her spine into the cushion.

"You know what happened." It was a statement rather than a question.

She shook her head.

"Don't fuck with me!" he screamed. "It's been on the radio, how I kidnapped my daughter." He laughed, a sinister, choking sound. "She's my *daughter*!" he thundered. "How can I be kidnapping something that's my own blood? She belongs to me."

Summer sat motionless. She thought maybe if she stayed still enough, she could melt away, just vanish from the room.

"I'm just trying to be a father," he said in a quieter voice. "Trying to keep my family together."

She wanted to vomit. A father? A family? This guy had no idea what he was talking about.

In the silence, her cell phone began to ring. T.J.'s head snapped in the direction of the bed stand. "Don't answer that," he growled.

"It's probably just Mac. He'll be here soon, usually comes by six or so." She hoped T.J. would believe the lie.

"What? Who?" Distracted, he edged toward a window, squinting outside.

"Mac. The guy who's working on the house."

Suspicion filled his eyes. "Thought Damian was working here."

"Well, they both are, but..."

Her phone stopped ringing.

"So where is he?" T.J. demanded.

His expression grew wild, and Summer realized the madman had come to the house looking for Damian. *Oh, God. Did he really mean to use the gun? How crazy was he? How drunk? How completely off the deep end?*

She swallowed. "I don't think Damian's working today."

T.J.'s eyes narrowed. "What do you mean?"

He's home protecting his mother from you, she wanted to say. *Or downtown at the police station, ready to lead a posse and find his sister, then capture your head on a stake.*

"He took the day off," she hedged. "I haven't seen him."

"Bullshit!" The gun wavered in his hand, and Summer jumped. T.J. strode to the bed stand and picked up her phone. One dirty thumb poised above the buttons. A grin peeled back his lips, and he shoved it into her hand.

"Call him. Tell him you need him to come over here and fix something. And do exactly what I say."

ᘓ᠀ᘔ

Damian took a long shower and let the hot water ease away some of his tension. Though it was barely six, he couldn't pretend to sleep anymore. He was exhausted, and not just because he'd lain awake on the couch waiting to hear news of Dinah. Whenever he closed his eyes, he thought of Summer. Of her house, of a sunset, of a guitar playing notes and starlight blinding him. She'd been barefoot in the dream, wearing that damn sundress cut clear down to forever, and she'd chased him through the house, up to the roof, where she'd stopped and held out one hand to him. He'd taken it, wrapped his fingers around hers, and they'd started to float.

He lathered and rinsed until the water turned cool. Maybe his mother was right. Maybe he could find the words to tell Summer about the way she twisted him up inside. But she was leaving, he reminded himself. What good would it do to spill his guts and then watch her get on a plane bound for the opposite coast? *Forget it.*

Downstairs, he gulped black coffee and called the precinct.

"Heard anything?"

"Nothing yet. Sorry. We're starting up a search again in another half hour or so."

"I'll be there."

He peeked in on his mother, who was sleeping. *Thank God.*

He turned over his cell phone in his palm. He itched to call someone—anyone—just to get rid of the thoughts inside his head. He'd decided on Cat and was about to punch in the numbers when the phone rang. One look at the Caller ID and his throat closed up.

"Hello?"

For a moment, there was only static and the faint sound of

breathing.

"Summer?"

"Damian." Her voice sounded strange and he could barely hear her. She drew in a sharp breath, and he thought he heard strange noises in the background. "Can you come over here? There's a problem with the plumbing in my bathroom and..."

"What?" Damian glanced at his watch. She'd called him for a plumbing problem? At dawn? "Um, I was gonna head down to the station in a few minutes. Isn't Mac gonna be there soon?"

Her voice lowered to a whisper. "He has a meeting over in Silver Valley first thing this morning." A knocking sound echoed in the background, and after a few seconds, Summer spoke again. Her voice was stronger this time. More detached. "Anyway, if you can just stop by for a few minutes and check it out, I'd really appreciate it."

"Um, I don't...maybe I could come by later on, before lunch." He frowned. No mention of the other night. No affection in her voice at all. Just a plumbing problem and a strange current of fear running across the telephone lines.

"Just for a few minutes?" she pleaded. "If you could—"

The line went dead.

છ૪ૐ

"Where the hell is he?" T.J. growled. He paced from one end of the bedroom to the other but kept the gun pointed at Summer. Every few minutes, he pulled back the curtains and peered through them.

"Maybe he isn't coming. He didn't say he would."

A sneer curled back the man's lips. "Oh, he's coming. For someone who looks as pretty as you, he'll show up. Always did like to play the big hero."

"But—" *He's angry with me. No, furious. Plus Dinah's still missing. That's more important than a broken toilet.* She didn't need to remind him about the little girl who'd gotten away. If T.J. was here with her, that meant he couldn't get to Dinah. Summer pressed her lips together and fought for strength.

The sun continued to rise, and the temperature in the room climbed. Perspiration slipped between her breasts and she wiped a hand across her forehead. A couple of cars drove by but none stopped. Her hopes dropped. What if Damian really didn't come? What if he decided that she could take care of her own problems? His little sister was missing, after all. Why on earth would a leak make him drop everything and rush to Summer's side?

Tears filled her eyes. It had been almost twenty minutes.

"He's not coming," she whispered. *Of course he's not. He blames you for letting T.J. get to Dinah. You announced to the world yesterday that you're leaving town. And if all that isn't enough, he spent last night with Joyce Hadley. He's not going to run over here and be your knight in shining armor.*

"Then you're gonna have to call him again." T.J. circled the room.

Summer wondered if he'd lost his mind. Her fear ratcheted up a couple of notches. A lonely father seeking revenge was one thing. A crazed man with a loaded weapon was something else altogether.

They both heard the noise at the same time, a sharp crack somewhere nearby. Summer jumped to her feet.

"Sit down!" T.J. hissed, waving the gun in her direction. "Stay right there and don't say a damn thing unless I tell you to." He crept to the bedroom door, brushing her bare knee. She cringed at the feel of his soiled jeans and sat back down.

"C'mon," he muttered. "I know you're out there." He stepped into the foyer and looked around.

Suddenly the front door flew open and Damian strode across the threshold. One fist shot out and punched T.J. in the mouth before the man had a chance to cock the gun. He stumbled against the wall. Blood poured from his split bottom lip.

Damian grabbed him by his shirtfront. Another punch. This time, though, T.J. ducked, and Damian's fist glanced off the wall. The skin on his knuckles split open, and Summer stifled a scream.

He came. Summer ran to the doorway and stopped. Damian's eyes flickered toward her, his gaze dark and pointed. She couldn't read it. Want? Blame? Uncertainty?

"You sonofabitch," T.J. slurred. He managed to push himself against the wall and straighten the gun. Squeezing the trigger, he fired.

Summer screamed.

Plaster erupted from a hole ten feet above Damian's head.

"Damn." T.J.'s grin slipped a little. He rearranged the gun in his hand as Damian lunged across the foyer. The hammer cocked.

Summer covered her eyes. She couldn't bear to look. The gun fired again, and then a third time. Grunts of pain filled the air. Something—or someone—thudded to the ground. Glass shattered. She kept her fingers over her face. "No," she whispered. Her legs trembled. "Please—"

A strong hand grabbed her wrist, and she cringed. Then the hand loosened a little and pulled her to her feet. She opened one eye. Then the other.

Damian Knight, whole and alive, smiled down at her.

CX80

"It's okay," Rachael was saying, but Summer couldn't hear her friend over her own sobs.

Rachael shoved another tissue into Summer's hand and slung an arm around her shoulder. She couldn't stop crying. Her chest heaved, and she leaned her head against her friend's. "I thought—"

"I know." For once, Rachael didn't say much.

Summer opened her swollen eyes and saw a collection of men in her front yard. T.J., who'd managed to shoot himself in the foot, lay strapped to a stretcher. Two cops and a medical technician hovered over him. Damian stood a few feet away under the oak tree, talking to a state trooper. Summer watched him with a heart so full it ached.

"How did you know?" she asked Rachael.

"Damian called us after he talked to you. Thought we should probably have the police come over here, just in case."

"And you came too?" She looked at Cat, who stood near the hedges with his hands in his back pockets. His blond hair shone in the sunlight. *God, T.J. might have tried to shoot them both.* The thought sent her head spinning all over again.

"Well, of course we came," Rachael said. "You think we'd miss all the drama? Please."

Summer's breath hitched in her chest. Across the yard, the officer flipped his notepad closed and shook Damian's hand.

"Told you he was a keeper."

But Damian didn't look up at them as he stood in the lawn talking to his mother. "I don't know...I mean, I'm still leaving. I told everyone that. I don't have a reason to stay, really."

239

Summer stopped and remembered something else. "Besides, I saw him with Joyce Hadley last night. Outside Zeb's."

"So?"

"So they were *together*, Rach. I think the other night with us was—I don't know—just something that happened." *Something he probably regrets.* "Yeah, he came over here. But I asked him to look at my toilet. That doesn't mean he wants happily ever after with me." She looked down at her T-shirt and boxer shorts, torn from struggling with T.J. "I'm a mess."

Rachael leaned back. "How long are you gonna do this?"

"Do what?"

"You already stood up for a public stoning last night. You gonna turn into the martyr of Pine Point? You think you don't deserve any happiness because you made a mistake or two?"

Summer looked up, stunned. Rachael had never spoken to her like that. Never.

"Stop blaming yourself for everything that's ever gone wrong around here. You're not the reason T.J. took Dinah. You're not the reason Gabe spent time in jail."

"Maybe, but I—"

"You always said people had to come to terms with the past in order to understand the present," Rachael went on. "You've spent the last decade telling me that. But studying the past doesn't mean it defines the person you are forever, does it? It's just who you *were*. Not who you are."

Summer stared at her feet. All this time, Rachael had been listening.

The crowd in her yard thinned a little. For the first time, Damian glanced up at Summer, but she couldn't read his face.

"They're putting together search parties to look for Dinah. Want to help?"

Summer nodded. "Just let me shower first." She turned to head back inside and froze. Rachael's midnight message played inside her head. Was it possible? She stared at the house and then grabbed her friend's arm. "Wait."

"What?"

"I can't believe—I know where she is." Summer dashed inside. "I know where Dinah went."

"Wait a minute—what?"

"Get the police before they leave." Summer couldn't believe she hadn't thought of it earlier, right away. There was only one place in this town a scared little girl would go if her home had been violated and she didn't know where else to hide. Only one place safe enough to keep the bogeyman away.

And Summer knew exactly where it was.

⊰⊱

"Up on the third floor."

The policeman stood at her elbow and huffed onto the back of her neck as they climbed the stairs. He stopped Summer on the landing of the second floor. "Don't want you going any farther. Tell me where it is." His hand encircled her wrist and pulled her to the side.

But she stood her ground. "I have to go up. She'll be scared. She might not..." Her voice trailed off as the front door opened. Damian, Hannah and a second policeman stepped inside. Damian rushed to the staircase, but the policeman put a hand on his arm and said something she couldn't make out. She looked at Hannah and then was sorry. The woman was barely holding herself together. Her lips moved, but no sound came out. In one hand she held a wad of tissues.

Summer turned. She hoped she was right. She had to be

241

right. "It's on the next floor up. Back bedroom." *She was here the whole time...*

One more flight and they reached the closed door. The cop put a heavy hand on Summer's shoulder. "I want you to stay back."

She chewed her bottom lip but stayed where she was. Damian and Hannah hurried up the stairs. The policeman stepped inside the bedroom. Summer held her breath and counted to ten. Twenty. When she reached twenty-two, the man stuck his head back out into the hall and said in a low voice, "Come on."

Morning light shot the room with gold, and despite the dust everywhere, the walls glowed. She pointed, but she didn't need to. A black seam ran along the back of the far wall. The hidden door remained open a little more than an inch. Summer's heart nearly broke. *Poor thing.* Dinah had gotten it open but then hadn't managed to close it again. In the quiet, they could hear soft sobs.

"Dinah Knight?" The cop spoke first. His voice was kind. "It's okay, sweetheart. I'm a policeman. I'm here to make sure you're safe." He took a few steps toward the door, but no one answered.

"Ladybug?" Damian's voice broke on the word. "Are you in there?"

For another second they heard nothing but silence.

"Dame?" Dinah slid open the door and came running across the uneven floor at full tilt. Her arms reached out for her brother. Tears wet her cheeks, and both braids had come undone from their ribbons. Her eyes, pale moon saucers, darted from side to side, and she stumbled in her bare feet and called his name again.

In an instant he swept his sister into his arms. "It's okay, ladybug. I've got you. It's okay." Clutching her to his chest, he rocked back and forth, murmuring the words into the top of her head. "It's okay. It's all over."

Summer pressed trembling fingers to her mouth. Tears dampened her cheeks, but she didn't bother to wipe them away. For a moment she felt dizzy, and she wondered if another memory of the accident would knock her off her feet. It didn't. Strangely enough, she hadn't had a single flashback in over a day. Of course, they weren't hidden pieces of a whole any longer.

"Son of a bitch," the cop said as he stepped inside the hidden room. "Always heard about these things but never saw one before." He pushed his hat back on his head and kneeled. "Must-a been pretty small slaves to hide in a space like that." He looked over his shoulder. "That's what it was for, right?"

"Yes." Summer thought about telling him that slaves hadn't been that small, just desperate. And the ones traveling on the Underground Railroad had suffered far worse conditions than a warm, dry, ten-by-ten space in an isolated house this close to the Canadian border.

"Well, I'll be damned." He creaked up again and both knees popped. "Wait 'til the guys at the station hear about this." He radioed an all-clear down to his partner. "She okay?" he asked Damian. "Gotta get a statement from her if she's able."

Damian didn't speak. He just cleared his throat and moved into the hallway. Summer reached out to pat Dinah on the back, but she only brushed the wrinkled cotton shirt before Damian negotiated the two flights of stairs with his sister in his arms. Once they were back on the ground floor, Hannah swept her daughter into her arms with sobs and hysterical laughter.

"Oh, God. My baby...my baby...thank you..."

Summer descended with slow footsteps. By the time she

reached the foyer, the heavy front door had shut behind the Knights. Hannah, Dinah and Damian—a ring of three, a closed circle, a family that didn't include her. Her fingers rested on the smooth cherry banister until she slid to the first step and sat there, hugging her knees. She swallowed and tried to dislodge the lump in her throat. She'd gone to sleep in Damian's arms. She'd woken with the tip of a dream on her tongue that in the daylight had found truth after ten years of hiding. She'd talked to Gabe. She'd talked to the police. She'd helped find Dinah.

Summer wondered if it were possible to live an entire lifetime in a single day and night.

Chapter Twenty-Three

Damian sat on the bottom porch step with Dinah beside him.

"I was only a little scared when Dad took me away from the house," she was saying. "I didn't know where we were going and why you couldn't come too. He said if I was good and didn't cry, we could be a family again." She sat up and her eyes welled. "But he lied."

"I know, ladybug." Damian stroked the back of her hair and tried to contain his anger. "I know. The important thing is that you're back here with us now." Even as he comforted her with one hand, he squeezed the other into a fist. *What kind of father steals his child away? Then loses her in the middle of the night?* The only thing keeping Damian sane was knowing that T.J. was on his way to a long prison sentence.

"Summer told me about that secret room," Dinah whispered. "She said it was a place where people used to hide." She smiled.

Damian hugged her. "Then it was very smart of you to go there." His voice broke. *Summer told me about that secret room...*

There's a whole life out there, starting with someone on the other side of those trees who's waiting for you to come to your senses...

He squeezed his sister's thin frame. "Ladybug, run over to

Mom, okay? I'll meet you in just a minute. But there's something I have to do first."

◌℥℥◌

Rachael yawned and leaned against the banister next to Summer. "I need a nap. What time is it?"

"Um...seven. Ten after." She couldn't believe it. The sun had barely broken over the hills, and they'd already captured a criminal and saved a little girl.

"Call me later, okay?"

"You're leaving?" Summer wasn't sure her legs would hold her if she walked outside. "Don't yet. Stay for a while, would you?"

"I'll be back. Just tell me what happens," Rachael said as she pulled open the front door.

"What are you talking about?" Then Summer saw him standing at the foot of the porch steps, and she knew. Unshaven, exhausted, with a bruise rising on his jaw, Damian Knight was still the most attractive man she had ever seen.

She took in a deep breath and moved down the stairs until she stood on the step above him. Here they met almost eye to eye. Electricity jumped between them. She lifted her chin. *You saved me. You risked your life.* He could have stayed far from the house or left her alone to deal with the problem. But he hadn't. She wanted to embrace him, thank him, love him.

Blue eyes met hers and dropped away. "So you're leaving?" He ran both hands through uncombed hair. He didn't cross the space to touch her. Neither did he walk away.

Tension stretched between them, thin and taut, filled with everything that had happened the last time they'd been this close.

She couldn't speak. Yes. She meant to leave. That was the plan, after all. Sell the house and return to her home out west. Yet somehow, after everything that had happened in the last twenty-four hours, the plan seemed to have lost its appeal. In fact, it made no sense at all.

...studying the past doesn't mean it defines the person you are forever, does it? It's just who you were. Not who you are...

...it's the stuff of history books and museum exhibits. It shouldn't be the way we frame our lives. Learn from it, and then let it go. The present, and best of all, the future, well, that's up to us...

They're right, she thought suddenly. Once the past floated its way into memory, once people died, houses crumbled, kisses grew cold with a new dawn, no amount of wishing or years of study could bring it back. Or change it. It was what you did with the now that mattered.

"Were you going to say goodbye?"

Summer's gaze moved to the mountains beyond his shoulder. "I didn't see any reason to stay," she whispered. "After what happened with T.J. and Dinah, and then I saw you with Joyce, and I thought..."

"You thought what?" Damian crossed his arms, and Summer thought the dimple on his left cheek popped.

"I just figured..."

He wrapped his hands around her waist and pulled her close. "Can I tell you something?"

She nodded.

His mouth twisted a little. "Joyce is a good person. She was there for me when I needed someone to talk to. She listened." Damian took a deep breath. "But I've been waiting for you since before I knew you, Summer Thompson. Since the day you got into town. Since the moment you tripped down those back stairs. There hasn't been anyone else in the world for me since that day. Whatever you saw with Joyce, whatever you thought...it means nothing."

One rough thumb stroked her cheek, and a longing wider than the heavens swept between them and knotted up her insides. Sparklers went off inside her skull, inside every pore, and she wondered if he could feel it too.

"Damian..." Summer began, and then he was there, meeting her mouth with his. Sparks flowered, flooded, turned from pale yellow to brilliant orange and red until she saw a blazing rainbow of passion behind her eyelids. She clung to him and wound her fingers through his. She wanted to swallow him up so that her insides burned with sated desire. Tasting him, she drank in the sweetness and wanted it to go on forever.

In Damian's touch she was safe. More than that, she was swept away, up toward the clouds and beyond, to a place she'd never imagined existed. His hands moved along her spine, down her arms, raising gooseflesh. When he finally leaned back from her to breathe, she didn't want to let him go.

Damian's breath was a rasp of emotion. "Stay here in Pine Point. Please. I can't let you go. I won't." His voice was guttural; his eyes roved her face, searching for the answer he needed to find. "We all love you—Dinah, and Mom, and...and me too." He smiled. "Summer Thompson, I think I'm crazy in love with you. So please. Stay." The last words whispered away, and he crushed her lips with his again.

Summer wasn't sure if the warmth she felt on her back was the sun rising above them or the blood spinning her head around. Damian parted her lips with a tongue that needed, wanted, poured out possibility. He caressed the nape of her neck and the small of her back.

The girl of eighteen she'd once been, scared of the universe, injured almost beyond repair, felt her heart move up to the top of her head until she thought she would explode with pleasure. Every reason she'd returned to Pine Point, every hope she'd nourished, lay here, in the arms of a man she'd just met and yet known forever. Revisiting the past didn't mean going down old paths, then, but saying goodbye to them and forging new ones. Her mind swelled with the realization.

"Summer." The word was a breath against her cheek.

Don't stop kissing me, she wanted to say. *Take me upstairs, climb with me to the roof, show me the stars or the sun or the way the wind moves through the grasses on the hill. I don't care. Just be with me.*

"What?" she said instead.

Damian didn't answer. He just looked down at her with a kind, funny grin, and she saw in his expression the place where she wanted to stay, to make a life and grow a love. He met her mouth with his, touched tongue to tongue in a whisper of desire, and their embrace changed again, from a fire against the sky to a warm glow that bathed her in safety.

Her friends were right after all: she belonged in Pine Point with a man who loved her, a little girl she adored and a quiet woman who'd filled an ache in her life. She belonged in the place that had shaped her, and she belonged in a house where she could see and remember her brother as well.

There was just one thing left to do.

"Wait." She dropped his hands and moved away.

He frowned. "What is it? What's wrong?"

Summer shook her head as she darted back into her bedroom. *He'll understand.* Emerging with the small silver box, she reached for his hand and led him to the oak tree out front. The sky opened above them, a wide plain of light. Summer's

249

hands shook as she opened the lid. *Thanks for bringing me back to Pine Point, Dad.* Her throat clogged with tears.

The morning breeze lifted her father's ashes. They spun, then sank in a lazy circle and floated to the ground. With one arm around her waist, Damian brushed a kiss against her hair. He laid a hand on hers, and they closed the lid of the box together. For a moment, neither spoke.

Damian cleared his throat. "So does that mean you're staying?"

She didn't answer. She had no words left beyond the flood of emotion that filled her. Instead, she placed her lips against his jaw and let her head fall against his chest, strong, certain, safe, beneath her.

It is home, she thought in the seconds before Damian lifted her into his arms and carried her back inside.

I am home.

About the Author

When Allie Boniface isn't writing about the power of love or exploring the complexities of the human heart, she's working as a high school English teacher in the northern NYC suburbs, where she lives with her husband, Todd. To learn more about Allie, please visit www.allieboniface.com.

Can anything change in 24 hours? Can everything?

One Night in Napa
© 2009 Allie Boniface
A One Night story

Journalist Grant Walker has one chance to salvage his job and his relationship with his domineering father. When terrorists kidnap a fading film star's son, he's there to get the first interview with a grieving mother. Even better, her illegitimate granddaughter arrives on the scene—a granddaughter who hasn't been heard from in seven long years. It's the story of a lifetime, and all Grant has to do is deliver.

Kira March left her childhood home seven years earlier, vowing never to return after discovering a terrible secret about her birth. But when her father is taken hostage and her adoptive grandmother cracks under media pressure, it's up to Kira to find and destroy all evidence of that secret. Trouble is, a reporter has weaseled his way into the house looking for answers—and he isn't leaving until he gets them.

As the hours pass, Kira finds herself falling for the very man who can destroy her. And when Grant comforts her in the wake of a midnight tragedy, he discovers that reporting a story gets a lot more complicated when you have feelings for your interview subject. As dawn nears, both Kira and Grant are forced to examine the ways in which their fathers have shaped them—and the lengths they'll go to protect and uphold the family name.

Available now in ebook and print from Samhain Publishing.

*Before she can build a future,
she must dig up the bones of her past...*

Uncovered

© 2009 Linda Winfree

A Hearts of the South story

After nearly twenty years, her career in possible ruins, homicide detective Madeline Holton returns to her hometown for a temporary stint working with the local sheriff's department. The demons of her teen years lie in wait, rising once more in the form of a cold case she must solve. And when it comes to a handsome farmer who's making good on her family's former land, she can't seem to keep her foot out of her mouth—or her hands off him.

Agricultural businessman Ash Hardison won't lie to himself—despite Madeline's obvious issues, he's more drawn to her than any woman he's ever known. He's already laid the ghosts of his past to rest, and he's determined to help Madeline purge hers. Whether she likes it or not.

Because he knows it's the only way they have a chance to forge a future together.

Warning: Contains deadly secrets, a prickly heroine and a determined man who knows what he wants.

Available now in ebook and print from Samhain Publishing.

One workaholic. One gigolo. One week in Sin City.
You do the math...

Bait and Switch
© 2009 Ann Lory
Frisky Business, Book 1

Anna Jackson's ex-boyfriend may have stolen her promotion, but she's not mad. Not anymore. She's getting even—by beating him at his own game. So what if she has to give up all her free time and any semblance of a personal life? With a partnership in a law firm as prestigious as Beckam, Beckam and Leland on the line, she's willing to pay the price.

Las Vegas escort Devon McGuire is charming, sexy, and damn good at pleasing women. He'd better be, it's what he gets paid for. Always up for a challenge, he's looking forward to his newest job. Who wouldn't enjoy a week as the companion of a smart, sultry, high-powered attorney—no strings attached?

Devon's used to pushing boundaries, but there's something about Anna that makes him want to turn up the steam. And when she learns to let go and unexpectedly opens to him, he finds himself falling right in.

Whoa, hold it. *Love* was never part of the plan...

Warning: This book contains a sizzling, drop-dead gorgeous, sex-on-a-stick gigolo who wants to make women's fantasies come true, and a woman who won't cooperate and let him do his job.

Available now in ebook from Samhain Publishing.

hot stuff

Discover Samhain!

THE HOTTEST NEW PUBLISHER ON THE PLANET

Romance, fantasy, mystery, thriller, mainstream and
more—Samhain has more selection, hotter authors, and
everything's available in ebook.

Pick your favorite, sit back, and enjoy the ride!
Hot stuff indeed.

WWW.SAMHAINPUBLISHING.COM

GREAT
CHEAP
FUN

Discover eBooks!

THE FASTEST WAY TO GET THE HOTTEST NAMES

Get your favorite authors on your favorite reader, long before they're
out in print! Ebooks from Samhain go wherever you go, and work with
whatever you carry—Palm, PDF, Mobi, and more.

LaVergne, TN USA
15 November 2010
204929LV00003B/1/P